The Mysterious Visitor

The Mysterious Visitor

A LION AND BOBBI MYSTERY

Joan Weir

POLESTAR

An Imprint of Raincoast Books

Polestar Books and Raincoast Books gratefully acknowledge the support
of the Government of Canada through the Book Publishing Industry
Development Program, the Canada Council and the Department of
Canadian Heritage. We also acknowledge the assistance of the Province
of British Columbia through the British Columbia Arts Council.

Cover design by Ingrid Paulson
Cover art by Ljuba Levstek

NATIONAL LIBRARY OF CANADA CATALOGUING IN PUBLICATION DATA

Weir, Joan, 1928–
   The mysterious visitor

   ISBN 1-55192-504-4

   I. Title.
PS8595.E48M95 2001   jC813'.54   C2001-910859-1
PZ7.W44My 2001

Polestar, an Imprint of Raincoast Books
9050 Shaughnessy Street
Vancouver, British Columbia
Canada, V6P 6E5
www.raincoast.com

1 2 3 4 5 6 7 8 9 10

Printed and bound in Canada by Webcom

With sincere thanks to my son Paul, for his legal advice and assistance, to the staff at the B.C. Ministry of Water, Land and Air Protection for their advice and cooperation, and to my daughter-in-law Jacqueline, who first taught me about crop circles.

Chapter 1

"What's wrong?" Lion asked, glancing sharply at his sister Bobbi.

Half an hour ago she'd come back from grooming the horses down in the pasture and had ever since been sitting in frowning silence, a puzzled, almost uneasy, look in her eyes.

For the first little while, Lion had been too busy watching the clock and worrying over how he was going to tell Dad about the baseball he'd just put through the kitchen window to think about his sister. But at last her funny mood penetrated. "What is it?" he asked again.

For a minute Bobbi continued to stare into space, then her glance came back. "I'm wondering about a girl I saw in the pasture. I probably wouldn't even have noticed her, except that all of a sudden a funny sort of wind started blowing and I looked around to see why. She was just standing there. I got this really strong feeling that she wanted to speak to me, so I started toward her. It was weird because as soon as I started to move, the wind seemed to die down. Only then I heard a car coming down the highway. I thought it might be

Dad, so I glanced around, and when I turned back, the girl had disappeared."

"Obviously she thought it was Dad coming home, too," Lion said with a grin. "She knew she had no business being in our pasture, so she took off."

"But there wasn't time!"

"Then she must have decided to hide in the deep grass or behind some bushes. You'd hide too if you were on someone else's property and the owner suddenly arrived home."

"I suppose." Bobbi didn't sound convinced. "She looked about sixteen or seventeen, wearing jeans, a shirt and one of those floppy sou'wester hats." Pausing, Bobbi looked up, then added quietly, "It was more than just a feeling that she wanted to talk to me, Lion. I was almost positive that something was wrong … that she was worried or scared or in some kind of trouble, and that's why she'd been trying to catch my atten—"

"Come on, Bobbi!" Lion interrupted firmly, trying to hide the sudden alarm he was feeling. "Every time you get one of those funny feelings of yours, we both end up in trouble. Last time, up in Powell River, we practically got ourselves drowned in that octopus spawning bed. What's strange about some girl driving by, seeing the horses and deciding to stop and pat them?" He deliberately kept his voice matter-of-fact.

"Nothing," Bobbi countered. "Except that I didn't see any car, or anybody walking away."

"So, she was probably hidden by a bush or by a drop

in the ground or something. Stop worrying, okay?" Again Lion glanced at the clock. "Instead, tell me what I'm gonna say to Dad about that broken window."

While Bobbi had been down in the pasture, Lion had been playing ball on the front street. The game had ended abruptly when he'd put the ball through their kitchen window. It had been a terrific hit. If they'd been in the park or on the schoolyard it would have been a home run for sure. But Dad had made it clear years ago that baseball wasn't a game for the front street. As soon as he arrived home from his law office, Lion was going to have to explain how he happened to overlook that ruling, and he still hadn't decided …

It was too late. Dad's car could be heard pulling into the driveway.

Bracing his shoulders, Lion waited. It was only the first of August, but already he could see this was shaping up to be another of those bad months for kids. There were a lot of them in a year, he'd discovered. About twelve, as a matter of fact — if you happened to be using the Roman calendar.

Dad came through the doorway.

Determined to get it over with, Lion blurted quickly, "I'm really sorry, but I broke the kitchen window with a baseball. It was an accident."

He waited for the axe to fall.

For a moment it seemed his words hadn't even registered. Then Dad said in a vague, preoccupied tone, "Broken windows will have to wait. Right now it's the threat of broken friendships that is worrying me." Without another word he moved across the hall and disappeared into his study.

Lion felt himself go limp with relief. Maybe he wasn't going to have to spend the last month of summer vacation on a short leash after all. In which case, maybe August wasn't going to be as bad a month for kids as he'd thought.

"Depend on it," Bobbi's amused voice broke into his thoughts. "Sooner or later Dad will get back to that window. Don't count your chickens yet."

Lion's grin widened. As usual his sister had guessed what he was thinking. She was uncomfortably good at that. She was also uncomfortably good at forecasting what was going to happen. Sooner or later Dad *would* get back to that broken window, but who cared about sooner or later? He could worry about sooner or later when sooner or later came. All that mattered at the moment was right now, and right now everything was great. The world was revolving exactly as it should. He wasn't in trouble with Dad over the window, and his sister had forgotten all about that zany girl in the pasture.

Whistling cheerily, Lion moved into the living room to check out the TV listings before dinner.

Chapter 2

Dad didn't come back out of his study until supper was ready. He sat down at his place, helped himself to some chili and rice and sat staring at it, not even picking up his fork.

Lion watched from under half-lowered eyelids. He'd seldom seen Dad so worried looking. What broken friendship could he have been talking about? Pushing back the shock of blond hair that as usual was falling forward over his forehead, Lion glanced across the table at his sister.

Bobbi was fourteen, two years older than he was, and particularly since Mom had moved out last year, Dad sometimes told Bobbi things about his law cases that he didn't share with Lion.

But from the quick shake of her head Bobbi gave him, it was obvious that this time she was just as much in the dark as he was.

In which case, he might as well eat, Lion decided, because chili was one of his favourites.

He'd almost finished his whole plateful before Dad finally looked up. "I have to go down into the south Okanagan for a few days on some rather upsetting business," he said, looking from Bobbi to Lion.

"It concerns a friend of mine. Brock Simpson. You've heard me talk about him. He owns a big ranch right in the middle of one of the most ecologically sensitive areas in all of Canada." Dad's face tightened. "For some reason some people from the Ministry of Water, Land and Air Protection suddenly seem to think he could be poaching endangered species."

Lion stared in dismay. No wonder Dad was upset. Wildlife was one of his favourite concerns. "Why would anybody poach endangered animals?" he protested.

"For money, obviously." Dad's voice was hard. "But there's something else as well. The authorities also seem to think they have uncovered evidence that Brock could be planning to sneak some of his best agricultural land out of the Agricultural Land Reserve and sell it illegally for housing lots."

"You mean you can't do that?" Lion asked.

"Not without government permission. Agricultural land is too valuable a natural resource."

Bobbi was watching Dad closely. "Has Mr. Simpson asked you to come down to help defend him against these charges?"

Dad's face tightened even more. "If he had, there'd be no problem. It's the Land Reserve Commission people who want me to go down to conduct the investigation against Brock." He looked away. "I tried to reach Brock on the phone before giving them my answer, but just as he came on the line something happened to the connection. The operator said it was some sort of wind interference, which didn't make sense to me. But the Commission people refused to wait for their answer. So, I had to agree to go without first talking to Brock." Seemingly unaware of what he was doing, Dad had picked up a magazine, wrapped it into a roll and was now twisting it between his hands. "If I go down there and start asking questions," he went on, his attention on the magazine. "Brock's going to think I don't trust him. How's that going to make him feel when I'm one of his closest friends?" A self-conscious note crept into his tone. "Particularly since he's always been there for me when I've needed a friend — like when your mother decided to move out."

"Then say you won't go," Bobbi replied quickly.

For the first time, the harsh lines of Dad's face relaxed slightly. "I thought of that. And if I'd been able to get through to Brock that's what I was going to tell him. But now I've realized if I don't go, the person the Land Reserve Commission sends may not try nearly as hard as I will to prove Brock is innocent." He brushed at some lint on the sleeve of the suit jacket he was still wearing from his day at the office, then his expression softened. "So, I'm going to go down for a few days. And since it's still summer holidays, I'm wondering if you two might like to come with me." For the first time the hint of a smile pulled at the corners of his lips. "Particularly since I'm told that one of those strange crop circle formations has turned up in the area."

Lion's head snapped up. "Really?"

"If you mean is it really a crop circle, the answer is probably no." The smile widened. "I suspect it could be a prank by some of the students at Okanagan University College — a copycat kind of thing — like the stunts every year at the University of British Columbia when the Engineering students suspend a Volkswagen from a bridge or a building. But a lot of the people in the area are definitely intrigued. In fact, a surprising number are insisting that the circle could be genuine. You wouldn't believe how many interesting theories are being suggested by normally sensible people. A couple of them even claim to have seen a strange girl appearing and disappearing in the vicinity."

Out of the corner of his eye, Lion saw the sudden gleam of excitement in his sister's eyes. He knew she was trying to catch his attention, but he pretended not to notice. No way he was buying into any weird disappearing girl. But a crop circle formation was something else. That he'd really like to see. They'd gone with Dad on two other cases this summer, one to the Barkerville area and one to Powell River, but neither of them had included anything as far out as this. "Maybe while you're solving Mr. Simpson's problems," he said eagerly, "Bobbi and I can get the jump on all those fancy scientists and discover what really is causing those crop circle patterns."

"More important," Bobbi added with a saucy grin, "maybe we can discover if there really are space visitors."

Lion gave her a disgusted look.

To everyone's relief, Dad's gloom over his friend Mr. Simpson seemed to have lifted. He got to his feet. "Whether you decide to spend your time checking out crop circle patterns or whether you decide to go looking for space visitors, you'll need some way to get around, so we'll take the horses."

Lion's excitement took a nose dive. Investigating crop circle formations could involve a lot of travelling. If it did, and if they had to do all that travelling on those dumb horses …

Suddenly, he had an idea. In a deceptively innocent tone he asked, "Is the south Okanagan a pretty big area?"

Dad nodded. "With lots of isolated stretches."

"Then wouldn't it be better if Bobbi and I had something more dependable to get around on than horses?"

Dad had been about to move away from the table, but now he paused. "Perhaps it would," he agreed, his voice thoughtful. "Maybe you do need something more dependable."

Lion beamed delightedly. He should have spoken up against the horses long ago. Now the question was how to get Dad thinking on the same wavelength he was about neat, motorized trail bikes. With two of those, he and Bobbi could ride in comfort for as long and as far as they wanted. Also, trail bikes didn't argue about which trail to take, like certain horses he knew.

"What's the name of that good sporting equipment store that you're always talking about?" Dad asked, still looking thoughtful.

Lion beamed even harder as he gave Dad the name and address of the store that sold the best trail bikes in town. He wasn't going to have to plant the idea of bikes in Dad's head after all — Dad was already on that page. He'd pick an all black bike, Lion decided. Bobbi could have red or green or silver, but he'd have solid black. He pictured himself revving up his new bike and starting to climb this really steep hillside —

"We'll stop as we head out of town tomorrow morning," Dad promised. "Each of you can pick out whatever style and colour you want, but you've got to make sure they're sturdy and well made."

Lion nodded eagerly.

"Also, you've got to be sure they'll be useful over all different kinds of terrain," Dad went on.

Again Lion nodded.

"That's probably the most important thing to consider," Dad added, "when you're putting out a lot of money to buy new jogging shoes."

Bobbi burst out laughing.

Lion retreated in disarray. So much for thinking August might be any different from the other eleven months of the year.

Chapter 3

"I'd like to get started as early as possible tomorrow morning," Dad added, disappearing into his study.

Lion didn't even hear. He was still in shock after having his new trail bike disappear just as he was about to sit on it.

Bobbi grinned at him. "Forget the bike and help clear the dishes. Then we'd better go down to the pasture and load our stuff into the horse trailer."

With difficulty Lion pulled his thoughts back. "Why? There'll be lots of time in the morning."

"Maybe. But to be sure we should do it tonight." A funny self-conscious note had crept into Bobbi's voice.

"You don't care any more than I do about loading the trailer!" Lion accused, guessing the truth. "You just want to go down to the pasture to see if that girl is still there!"

His sister didn't even bother to deny it. "But at the same time," she added, "we can let the horses know that we're going."

Lion's eyes lifted skyward in disgust. "Which part do you figure they'll understand best? The bit about the disappearing girl, or the debate about patterns in crop circles?"

17

"Neither, silly." She put the last of the dishes into the dishwasher and turned it on. "But you know as well as I do that when the horses see us packing the trailer they'll guess something is up, and it's only fair to tell them they'll be coming too." Without waiting for an answer, she opened the kitchen door and led the way outside.

"As if horses can understand English," Lion muttered as he started after her. Some things his sister took too far. Explaining their plans to the horses was bad enough, but going back to check on that girl was way too far out for him. There couldn't have been anybody in the pasture in the first place — not if she disappeared in front of Bobbi's eyes. His sister had to have imagined it. To insist on going back out there now, when there was a *Mission Impossible* rerun on TV —

"But I didn't imagine it."

Lion jumped guiltily. Darn it all, that was another thing about his sister — the way she seemed to be able to guess what he was thinking. He wished she'd cut it out.

"She really was there," Bobbi continued. Then in a self-conscious rush she added, "And I think she's still there. Otherwise, why do I have this feeling that I've got to get back down there right away before —"

"Cut it out, Bobbi! Okay!" Lion protested quickly. He wasn't about to admit it, but his sister was making him uneasy. Not giving her a chance to say anything more, he set off at a rapid pace toward the pasture.

They lived on a small acreage just twenty kilometers outside of Vancouver. The house sat on a large treed lot

18

close to the highway, but behind the house extended five acres of large grassy pasture. At the top end of the pasture was a tack shack where they kept all their supplies. In the centre of the field was a roomy wooden horse shelter closed over top and down three sides for the horses to use in bad weather. Today, however, was bright and sunny, and both horses were grazing along the far fence line. At the sound of voices, their heads came up. They turned and stood watching.

"Brie! Come here, Brie!" Bobbi called continuing to move nearer. "I've something to tell you."

Lion grimaced in disgust.

Whinnying, Brie started toward them.

Bobbi directing a see-I-told-you-so look at Lion.

"Now I suppose you're going to pretend she understood that garbage about having something to tell her," he said disgustedly. "You know darn well the only reason she's coming is because she thinks you have a treat for her."

"Maybe," Bobbi conceded as Brie continued to approach. "But horses understand lots more than you give them credit for."

"Garbage. There's your proof." Lion nodded toward a big sorrel coloured Arabian gelding who, despite Bobbi's calling, continued to stand motionless. "If horses understood what you said about having something to tell them, Raj would be coming as well as Brie to find out what it was."

"No, he wouldn't. Because I didn't call him. I only

called Brie. Raj knows he's your horse, so he's waiting for you to call him."

"Well, I don't intend to."

"Then I will. Come on, Raj. Come on, boy!"

Immediately the big Arab started moving toward them. Reaching Bobbi, who was half a dozen paces ahead of Lion, he stopped beside her. He rubbed his head several times up and down her arm.

"Good boy," Bobbi told him, scratching behind his ears.

Raj glanced over at Lion, but he didn't move toward him. He waited.

"Tell him hello," Bobbi prompted.

"Hello, you dumb horse," Lion retorted.

For a second longer Raj studied him, then, lifting his tail high in the air as Arabian horses do, he turned and moved back the way he'd come.

"And you say horses can't understand what we say!" Bobbi fumed angrily. "Maybe animals don't understand words, but they understand tone of voice and meaning. How would you like it if every time you tried to be friendly to somebody they called you names?" Casting another furious glance at Lion she moved after Raj. "It's all right, boy," she called. "Come on, Raj."

But the big horse paid no attention. Dropping his head he went back to grazing.

For the first time Lion felt a pang of conscience. It was true. He did spend a lot of time telling Raj he was dumb and stupid and useless. But it was his own fault for being so pig-headed and independent, Lion reminded himself.

Then he remembered how Raj had come to his rescue when he was on the point of being shoved down that deserted mine shaft up in Wells. And how he helped save C.J. when they were with Dad on that case up in Powell River.

"So, I didn't mean it. Okay?" he called gruffly.

The big Arab's head came back up.

Swallowing his pride and pushing down his embarrassment Lion forced himself to continue. "I didn't mean it, Raj. You're not dumb. Actually, a couple of times you've been pretty helpful. So, okay?"

As Lion had been talking, Raj's ears had come forward, listening. For a minute he continued to watch Lion, then he blew down through his nostrils, tossed his head high in the air and lowered it again to the grass.

Lion's temper flared. "So much for you and your theories," he stormed at Bobbi, struggling to cover his embarrassment. Was he ever glad none of the guys had been around to hear him apologizing to a horse. What had he been thinking of to let his sister con him into doing anything so dumb? He just hoped she didn't tell anyone. But knowing Bobbi, he was sure she would. She'd think it was a huge joke. A guy could spend his whole life trying to live down something like that.

But instead of laughing, Bobbi was beaming. "Stop looking so embarrassed, silly. It worked! Raj heard you! Didn't you see the way he nodded his head? He under-

stood what you said, and he isn't hurt any more."
Seemingly satisfied that the subject was closed, she
pulled a brush out of the pocket of her jacket and turned
away to start polishing the dust off Brie's gleaming
chestnut-coloured coat.

Lion stared in disbelief. She couldn't really believe
the dumb horse had nodded! But now he'd never know
for sure that Raj *hadn't* understood — that he *hadn't*
nodded! Darn Bobbi anyhow!

But Bobbi's polishing brush had stopped in mid air.
She was staring across the pasture as if she'd just seen a
ghost. "Lion! Look!" she whispered. "I knew she'd be
still here! I knew she wouldn't leave without explaining
why she'd come!"

Quickly Lion looked where his sister was pointing.
But the rays of the setting sun were so bright it was
impossible to see clearly. His eyes kept filling with tears.
No sooner did he think someone was there than the picture faded away again. Impatiently, he brushed again at
his eyes.

Bobbi meantime was starting to run. But before she'd
taken more than a dozen steps, the loud blaring of a
truck horn sounded on the highway behind them, followed by a squeal of brakes. Startled, Bobbi glanced
back. Next moment she turned and started running
again, but after only two steps she stopped. "She's
gone!" she exclaimed in disappointment. "She was here
a moment ago! But now she's gone!"

The sun had dropped lower against the horizon. It

was no longer shining in Lion's eyes. He could see clearly. The pasture was empty.

He let his breath out in relief. He wasn't about to admit it to his sister, but he couldn't have been happier. He got really uneasy when his sister got one of her weird feelings, because her success rate for forecasting trouble or danger was just about a hundred percent. If she said she had a funny feeling that somebody was in danger, like she did about the witcher up at Wells and the Principal's kid in Powell River, then she meant it. She didn't joke about things like that. And she hadn't been joking this time. She'd really thought there *had* been a girl in the pasture and that for some reason the girl was in trouble. But the sun can play tricks when it gets in a person's eyes, Lion told himself firmly. Everybody has had that happen. Sure, Bobbi thought she'd seen someone, but as soon as the sun dropped a bit she'd realized there was nobody there after all.

Which meant, he told himself happily, starting back the way they'd come, if there was no girl, then there couldn't be any funny feelings about somebody being in danger. And if there were no funny feelings about anybody being in danger, then there was nothing for him to worry about.

He walked faster. If he hurried he could still catch some of that *Mission Impossible* rerun.

Chapter 4

"So, tell us more about where we're going," Lion said next morning as Dad maneuvered the station wagon with the horse trailer attached onto the feed-in lane joining the Trans-Canada Highway east.

To be honest, he wasn't all that interested in where they were going. All he really cared about was that neat crop circle — exactly where it had been sighted, for instance — how long it would take them to get there and what the local people were saying about it. But he didn't want to push that too soon in case Dad immediately set down ground rules. However, he had to say something because, if he didn't, in about two more seconds Dad would notice the way Bobbi was staring in preoccupied worry out the window and ask what was going on.

Lion knew of course that his sister was watching for a reappearance of that imaginary girl, and the last thing he wanted was for her to explain that to Dad. Particularly not if she went on and added the bit about having one of those feelings of hers that something was wrong. If Dad heard that, he might ground Lion and Bobbi at the ranch for the whole visit. "So tell us more about where we're going and why," he repeated.

For a moment Dad was too busy manoeuvring the station wagon and the trailer past a line of slow moving traffic to answer. Then he settled back in his seat. "We're going to one of the most ecologically fragile areas in all of Canada," he replied.

Crop circles and imaginary girls were temporarily forgotten. "Is that why the big concern about somebody poaching endangered species and trying to sell off ranch land for city lots?"

"Exactly. The triangle of land from Penticton south to the U.S. border is tiny compared with our whole land mass, but within that tiny area live more than thirty percent of Canada's endangered wildlife species."

"What kinds of wildlife?" Bobbi put in quickly.

"To name a few, the badger, the prairie falcon, the eagle, and the white headed woodpecker. They aren't only threatened; they're in danger of complete extinction. And they aren't the only species at risk. So are burrowing owls, great blue herons, bobolinks, big horn sheep, even mountain caribou."

"You mean it could already be too late?"

Dad nodded. "Particularly if people start sneaking land out of the Agricultural Land Reserve and turn it into city lots."

Before Lion could stop himself, he heard himself saying, "D'you think the poaching and the plan to build houses on good agricultural land could have any connection with the crop circle?"

It was a mistake.

Dad's amused glance met Lion's in the overhead mirror. "Since those other things have been going on for months and the crop circle appeared just a few days ago, I think it highly unlikely. As I've already said, I suspect the crop circle is a student prank — prompted by that TV program a while back."

Lion had seen that program too. It had shown two men making crop circles with boards and had planted the suggestion that this could explain all the other crop circles all over the world.

But Lion couldn't buy that. He could certainly accept that those two men had made those two circles and that maybe other people had made other ones. But he couldn't agree that it explained all the circles, for some of them had been made too quickly. It had taken all night for the men on TV to make theirs, but there was proof that some circles had appeared in less than an hour. Independent observers claimed to have passed fields of grain that had no trace of anything disturbing the normal growing pattern, then just forty-five minutes later passing those same fields again to discover intricate crop circle patterns.

He wanted to ask Dad about that. As far as he could see, no men with boards could make intricate crop circle patterns in just forty-five minutes then disappear again without leaving a trace of footprints or equipment or any hint that they had even been there.

Also, there was something else he wanted to ask Dad about. He knew his sister more than half believed what several really far-out scientists had suggested — that the crop circles could possibly have been formed by the radiation emitted from some sort of hovering air vehicle. The scientists claimed that would explain the perfect symmetry of the patterns and the fact that the shafts of grain were bent over about four inches above the ground, but not broken, so they continued to grow. Of course, there was no way *he* was gonna buy into that kind of hocus-pocus. Still, he wouldn't mind asking Dad what he thought about it.

Only not when his sister was listening, he decided, giving her a quick sideways glance. It would just start her off again about that girl she imagined she'd seen in the pasture. Better stick to the poaching. So in a bright voice he suggested, "Maybe Bobbi and I could ride around and try to turn up some clues as to who might be behind that poaching business — you know, who might be setting those illegal traps. After all, nobody pays much attention to what two kids are doing. Haven't you noticed on TV how it's almost always the kids who work out what's —"

He should have stuck with the crop circles.

Dad's face in the overhead mirror had tightened. "After being almost sealed down a mine shaft in Wells and nearly drowned in Powell River, I would think you'd be ready to follow the basic ground rules for behaviour when you come with me on a case." His voice was at its driest. "However, since you seem once again to be suffering memory loss, let me remind you. The effort someone seems to be making to divert land out of the Reserve is my concern, not yours. So is the poaching. You and your sister are to take no part in looking into either thing. Is that clear?" He waited for Lion to nod, then in a different voice added, "And tighten your seat belt."

Resigned, Lion sat back in the seat and tightened his lap belt. So much for that idea. But at least it had gotten Bobbi out of her weird mood. To Lion's relief, his sister was gazing around for the first time with real interest in the thickly treed mountain scenery.

"Why would the south Okanagan in particular have so many wildlife species at risk of extinction?" Bobbi asked, still thinking about what Dad had said a moment earlier. "Why is it different from most other places?"

"You'll see as soon as we get there," Dad replied. "Within a relatively small area there is an unbelievably varied mix of every possible kind of habitat and terrain."

"Like what?"

"Bench lands, flat grass lands, river banks, rocky ledges — and all are interdependent on all of the others. But the trouble is, it's such an attractive place to live, with such a moderate year-round climate, that the human population is putting the ecosystem and the wildlife at risk. The number of people in the area has more than quadrupled in the last twenty years, and the forecast is for even more rapid growth in the future. If that happens, it will be fatal to the ecosystem and the wildlife."

Bobbi continued to frown. "But why?"

"Because when new people come into an area, they buy land and do things like diverting a creek or a river which can have fatal repercussions on nesting fowl or migrating birds or land-burrowing animals. They can flood flatland to make an extra drinking pond for cattle, destroying essential food sources for migrating elk and deer and small animals. They can build a road across the natural migration paths of the wildlife, resulting in their inability to get from their winter home to their summer pasture, resulting in possible starvation. Even putting up fences in certain sensitive areas can be fatal if those fences break up the natural grazing area and so separate groups, within a species. Once animals are broken into small groups they are easy prey for predators; and if there aren't enough males in the group, it is impossible for them to breed properly."

As Dad had been talking, Bobbi's face had grown increasingly tight. "Why aren't we taught things like that in school? Why don't we have laws so people can't do those things?"

"There are some laws, but not nearly enough," Dad agreed. "We must make more, and we must do it soon, or it could be too late for most of our wildlife."

For a long moment after that they drove in silence.

Then in an effort to lighten the mood, Bobbi said brightly, "So, tell us about this man we're going to visit?"

"Only if you both promise not to play amateur detectives," Dad answered sternly. "The stakes this time are too high. If Brock Simpson isn't guilty of trying to sell off

29

some of his land illegally or of poaching endangered species, as I'm sure he isn't, then someone else has deliberately set him up to take the blame. And if someone else has set him up to take the blame, it's for a reason. They've got an agenda of their own, and they won't sit calmly back and do nothing if they think you or I or anybody else is starting to get too nosy." Again his glance met Lion's in the overhead rear-view mirror. "Nosy people could be permanently removed. Even if you do put baseballs through kitchen windows, I don't wish to see either you or your sister permanently 'removed'."

"But we'll be careful!"

"I'm afraid your understanding of the meaning of that word is different from mine."

"Come on, Dad! You know you needed us those other times. You even admitted it yourself!"

Dad's eyebrows lifted frictionally. In his driest voice he admitted, "Perhaps. But I promise you, I intend to struggle very hard not to fall victim to the same kind of weakness this time."

Chapter 5

Dad had said at the start that it would take them about five hours to reach the ranch. By the time they'd traveled for four hours, Lion was famished. They'd stopped two hours earlier, and he'd pigged out on a double cheeseburger with fries and a coke, but he was starving again.

"We'll be there in another hour or so," Bobbi objected. "Can't you wait?"

"We'll be there in less than an hour," Dad corrected, smiling across the front seat at her. "But we'd better stop and feed our starving passenger or he'll eat poor Brock out of house and home as soon as we get there."

At the next roadside restaurant, Dad pulled off the highway and up to the drive-through window. As soon as Lion's order had been filled, Dad moved the car into the parking lot and turned off the motor. "While you're demolishing that cheeseburger, I'm going to take a walk to stretch my legs," he announced.

He'd barely moved away from the car, when a sudden gust of wind took his hat sailing. With an exclamation of annoyance, he set out after it.

At the same moment Bobbi straightened. "Lion! Look!" She pointed in the opposite direction from the one Dad had taken. "There she is again. In that field over by that hill. Can you see her?"

This time there was no sunset blinding Lion's vision and he could. But after his sister's big build up, he felt a wave of disappointment. "Why the big fuss? She looks perfectly ordinary to me."

"It's not what she looks like," Bobbi returned, still staring eagerly at the girl in the distance. "It's the way she seems to be able to catch our attention without doing or saying anything — sort of just by concentration —" Abruptly Bobbi broke off and substituted in a low excited tone, "Or with that sudden wind! Don't you see? She must be the one doing that. It's how she caught my attention yesterday afternoon, and how she stopped Dad being able to get though to Mr. Simpson on the phone to tell him he wasn't coming. Now she's used it to send Dad off chasing his hat so she can attract our attention again! Only why, Lion?"

"Forget that dumb stuff about the wind," Lion blustered disgustedly. "Nobody can make the wind blow just because they want it to. But it's weird that she's turned up here. D'you think she could be following us?"

"She must be. For some reason she must really want Dad to go down to see Mr. Simpson."

Lion wasn't convinced. "Then where's her car?" he pointed out, looking all around.

"I don't think she has one. I already told you there was no sign of any car yesterday when I saw her in the pasture."

"Yeah, right. Why didn't I remember that." Lion's voice grew even more sarcastic. "She's travelling on foot, of course. After all, we've only come three or four hundred kilometres. Where's the problem?"

Bobbi gave him an amused look but continued to watch the girl in the distance. All at once her whole body took on a funny listening look.

"What's wrong?" Lion asked quickly.

Bobbi didn't answer. She continued to stare into the distance where the girl was standing.

"Come on, Bobbi!" Lion was getting distinctly uncomfortable.

Slowly, Bobbi's attention came back. Then, looking self-conscious, she admitted in an embarrassed voice, "Whoever that girl is, I'm positive she knows about the trouble Dad's friend Mr. Simpson is in — about the poaching and about somebody trying to turn agricultural land into city lots."

"How could you know that when you've never even talked to her!"

Bobbi looked even more self-conscious. "That's what's so weird. You're right, there isn't any way I could know when I've never talked to either her or Mr. Simpson. But somehow inside I just do." She gave Lion an even more self-conscious smile. "I also know that's why she came to the pasture last night — because she needs us to help."

"Well, if she does, she has a weird way of showing it," Lion said sarcastically. "Usually when people want

33

help they hang around long enough to explain what's wrong."

Bobbi ignored his sarcasm. "Don't you remember, it was only after someone else came along each of those times that she disappeared." Bobbi's voice grew more excited. "First that car honked, which I thought was Dad coming home so I turned to see, and the second time a big truck came roaring past. Maybe she disappeared because she didn't want to talk to me when somebody else could see her."

It was too much for Lion. He turned his eyes skyward in disgust. When his sister got into one of these moods, there was no point in arguing.

Bobbi was continuing to watch the girl in the distance. She was moving up the hill now, making her way through the deep pasture grass.

At the same moment, Dad reappeared at the back of the station wagon.

Whether Bobbi was right and the girl would disappear again now that Dad was back, Lion didn't wait to find out. Quickly he turned to Bobbi. "Let's not say anything about how that girl keeps turning up and seems to be following us, okay? Dad could decide she's somehow connected with his case and ground us."

Bobbi gave him a teasing grin. "At least let's not say anything till after we find out what's going on."

There was no time to argue. Dad had reached the side of the station wagon. Climbing in he started the motor and manoeuvred the car and horse trailer off the main road onto a gravel one, across a cattle guard, then down a winding hill. Another half hour's drive through lush green pasture brought them within sight of the freshly painted red and white buildings of Willow Creek Ranch.

But even before they reached the ranch yard, it was clear to all of them that something was terribly wrong.

Chapter 6

As Dad brought the station wagon to a stop, the ranch 4×4 could be seen disappearing toward the hills in the distance. Seconds later a blond-haired girl ran out of the barn, leading a saddled brown roan. Her face was grey with worry. Seeing the station wagon, she paused momentarily. "I'm sorry, I can't stop," she called in a tight, frightened voice. "There's been an accident. Dad's gone for the vet. I'm going back out to the pasture to do what I can for poor Epic till they get there. Please go into the house. We'll be back as soon as we can." Without waiting for an answer, she swung up into the saddle, put the horse into a gallop and moved away.

It was almost an hour before the 4×4 returned, a white faced, shaken Brock Simpson behind the wheel. At the sight of Dad sitting waiting on the ranch house steps, his face broke into a disbelieving smile. "Syd! You old son-of-a-gun! Where did you come from?" A second later he was pumping Dad's hand. "But what does it matter? The important thing is that you should suddenly turn up just when I need you most. Come in, come in!" As he spoke he led the way onto the house, one arm still around Dad's shoulders.

Bobbi and Lion followed.

Dad introduced Bobbi and Lion to Mr. Simpson, then he asked quietly, "What's wrong, Brock? Your daughter — at least I assume it was your daughter — said there'd been an accident … that you'd gone to get the vet."

Mr. Simpson nodded. The smile vanished from his face. In its place the sick, grey pallor reappeared. "To Epic. Our best jumper and top breeding stallion. I can't understand it, but somehow he got into some barbed wire."

"Just now?"

"No. Probably early this morning, but we just discovered it. By luck, Chrissy went to check on him. She hadn't intended to. But a sudden gusty wind came up, and knowing how spooky Epic gets in wind storms, she decided to ride across the pasture and make sure he was all right. She found him caught in barbed wire."

"Badly caught?"

Mr. Simpson nodded. "She managed to free him, but he'd been fighting for so long to try to free himself that he'd almost cut through one of the major tendons in his foreleg. It's slashed so deeply the vet isn't making any promises."

"You mean he thinks the horse could have to be destroyed?"

"It's a possibility. But he's hoping with careful nursing and lots of rest that the leg will heal. Though I don't think he expects Epic to be able to jump any more." For a moment Brock Simpson was silent as the enormity of what had happened finally seemed to sink in. "There used to be a vet here — a girl," he said at last in a funny, tight voice. "She just sort of arrived one stormy night. Some people said she wasn't a real vet because she didn't have the right papers, but she could heal animals that everybody else had given up on. If only she were still here ..."

"Why didn't she stay?" Dad asked.

"Some of the people made it clear they didn't want her — that she was a fraud. And I guess it finally got to her, because she just up and left. Nobody saw her go, but one morning her hut was empty."

"Because of what people had been saying?"

Brock nodded. "Though I've always suspected it had something to do with that sand hill, too."

"Sand hill?"

"On a section of government land just beyond the end of our property. Actually, it's an old garbage dump. She'd been trying to get people to be concerned about it, because she suspected that over the years people had ignored the warnings and buried things there like old batteries and half empty paint cans and cleaning solutions. And she could have been right, because the strange thing is that not even weeds will grow there any more. It's just dry, dead, shifting sand."

"We're back, Dad!" called a voice from outside. Next moment the girl they'd seen briefly a while earlier appeared in the doorway. "We loaded Epic into one of the horse trailers, like you said, and brought him back to the barn in easy stages. The vet's getting ready to close all those awful cuts and gashes, and wants me to stand by and give poor Epic a little reassurance."

Mr. Simpson nodded. "If you need help, call me."

With a nod the blond-haired girl disappeared.

"I'm sorry, I should have introduced you," Brock Simpson said, running a worried hand through his hair. "I'm not thinking too clearly. That's my daughter, Chrissy."

"You couldn't be expected to think too clearly after what has just happened," Dad said quickly. "And if you want to go down to the barn too, don't worry about us. We'll sit here and relax."

Mr. Simpson shook his head. "I'd just be in Fergus' way down there. He just needs one person to calm and reassure Epic while he's working on him, and Chrissy is better at that than anybody." Again he fell silent, then, shaking his head as if to try to clear his thinking and speaking more to himself than to the others, he continued, "It's another of those freak accidents. I can't believe the bad luck we've been having. It seems to have been just one thing after —"

Abruptly he broke off, as if recalling his duties as host, and with forced cheerfulness said instead, "But enough of that. The important thing is that you turned up, Syd, just when I needed you most. Are you going to be able to stay for a few days? Have you come on business or pleasure?"

Quickly Lion glanced over at Dad, for that was the question he knew Dad had been dreading. By the time Dad had explained why he'd come, Brock Simpson's face was white with naked hurt and disbelief.

Dad was obviously shaken. "I told them I wouldn't come," he managed in a voice Lion hardly recognized. "I told them I wouldn't insult you by even asking questions, but they wouldn't listen." The words dried up.

The bleak look in Brock Simpson's eyes grew even more pronounced. "So, what do you want to know, Mr. Crown attorney," he said bitterly. "Or are you so convinced I'll lie that you aren't even going to bother asking questions?"

"Brock! You know it's not like that! Please?"

The anguish in Dad's voice made Lion wince.

And miraculously, Brock Simpson must have heard it too. The hurt faded from his face. "You do believe in me, don't you? You're doing this because you figured somebody else might not try hard enough to find out the truth." It was a statement not a question. "You don't believe I'm guilty of those things they're suspecting me of."

"Thank you," Dad managed in a gruff voice that Lion had never heard before, brushing a hand across his eyes as if some sort of mist had come into them.

Mr. Simpson must have noticed that mist too, for he moved closer and gave Dad's shoulder a firm squeeze. "I'm the one who should thank you." He coughed as if to clear his voice, then went on, "So what can I tell you?"

"Why the Land Reserve Commission would suddenly suspect that a successful ranching operation like this one would be in financial difficulties."

"Because we are," Simpson answered simply. "In the

spring I had to take out a large bank loan, and it looks as if I might have to take out another one this fall."

Dad stared in disbelief.

"To make matters worse," Brock Simpson continued, "somebody using my name has been making inquiries about the procedure for selling-off some of our land."

Dad tried to hide his concern. "At the Land Office?"

"And at the bank as well." Simpson's voice hardened. "Immediately, both the Land Office and the bank were onto me because, you know as well as I do, you can't just start selling off agricultural land. They thought I was trying to sneak it by, and I think for a minute they were even considering taking some sort of legal action — at least a stiff fine. Fortunately, somebody saw the person making the inquiries, and though they didn't know who it was, they did know it wasn't me and spoke up in my defense. But it's caused a lot of bad feeling. I'm not sure the bank would give me another loan now if I did need one."

"Surely they must have some idea who made those phony inquiries," Dad protested. "What about those sophisticated ID cameras that they say are supposed to be keeping a record of everything that goes on?"

For the first time Brock Simpson's stern expression relaxed slightly. "Actually they did get ID head shots of the person making the inquiry, only as luck would have it, that person was wearing a hat and carefully kept his head turned away so the details of his face were too indistinct to be recognizable."

"You've never had to take out a bank loan before," Dad was continuing in a puzzled voice. "Why have things suddenly gone wrong?"

"Partly because beef prices have been down, but mainly because of the string of weird and unexpected accidents that I mentioned a moment ago. The early ones coming one right after the other had pretty well wiped out our cash balance, and now this accident to Epic could put us in serious trouble. His success in the jumping ring has always brought in a steady demand for stud services. This year in particular we've been depending on that money from stud fees. Without it …" The words tailed off.

"You said there had been a series of accidents," Dad said, his voice even and matter-of-fact. "What kind of accidents?"

"First, some sort of virus struck a lot of the cattle. Then, a drinking pond went sour. We only lost a few head, but almost all the livestock dropped weight, which made a huge difference last fall in the cattle sales profits. Then this spring, for no reason at all, both the tractor and the bailer suddenly developed major problems and had to be replaced, which meant a huge cash outlay. Now this accident to Epic."

"I suppose there's always a certain degree of danger," Dad began, "when you use barbed wire around livestock —"

"But we never use it!" Mr. Simpson interrupted. "That's the strange thing! We've never allowed barbed wire to be used anywhere on the ranch, even in my father's day. This roll must have been lying there out of sight and forgotten for more than thirty years. The thick bracken in that area and that thick patch of wild roses must have hidden it. But still, you'd think one of us would have noticed."

Lion glanced over at Dad in time to see the lines of his face tighten. Was Dad wondering if some of those accidents might have been deliberate?

"Without Epic bringing in stud fees," Mr. Simpson admitted honestly, continuing to meet Dad's eyes with his own steady gaze, "I may have to arrange another loan — if I can get one that is. But it could finish us." His lips pulled into a lopsided smile. "You know what modern-day interest rates can do to a business's financial picture, so I won't rush in. I'll hold off as long as I can. But if we have any more bad luck … " He left the sentence hanging.

For a second Dad's attention seemed to be needed to brush some lint from the leg of his trousers. Then in a deliberately non-worried tone he remarked, "Getting back to those bank ID shots, d'you think a good photographer could bring the prints up enough that you could see some details about the person making the inquiries? If we could see anything that would help us identify who that person is so that we could —" Abruptly he broke off, for someone was standing in the living room doorway.

Several moments earlier Lion had heard the front

43

door open and footsteps come across the hall. Since neither Dad nor Mr. Simpson had felt the need to break off their conversation, he'd assumed it must be Chrissy coming back from looking after Epic. Now, however, both men were staring in startled dismay at a stocky, dark-haired man in jodhpurs and black English riding boots who was standing at the entrance to the living room. He held a leather riding crop in one hand and was unconsciously flicking it against the side of one boot as he stood staring at them. The noise seemed unnaturally loud in the sudden silence.

How long had be been listening? Lion wondered. Had he overheard what Dad and Mr. Simpson had been talking about? He waited for Mr. Simpson to say something.

Instead it was the newcomer who broke the silence. "Sorry, I should have knocked." The words were clipped and abrupt. "I didn't realize you had company." He focused his attention on Brock Simpson. "I've just been having a look at those young jumpers of mine that your daughter is schooling for me. How soon does she think they'll be ready for my girls to start riding?"

"Almost any time," Brock Simpson replied, still noticeably off balance. "I think Chrissy feels both jumpers are sufficiently well disciplined and controlled."

"Then I'd like to start the girls' lessons the day after tomorrow."

Mr. Simpson nodded.

The newcomer turned to go.

"Oh, Syd, this is a neighbor of ours," Mr. Simpson put in almost as an after thought. "Warren Montcrief. He owns the property across the way."

Dad got to his feet to shake hands. A moment later the jodhpur-clad figure excused himself and disappeared back into the hall.

"I'd as soon Montcrief hadn't heard what we were saying about those ID pictures," Mr. Simpson said as the front door closed. "The fewer people who know about them the better. But it's nothing to worry about. Montcrief is a neighbour and a friend. I'm sure he won't say anything about them to anyone else."

"Just the same, I'd put them some place safe," Dad cautioned. "At this point they're your only link with whoever is trying to cause trouble."

Brock Simpson nodded. "They'll be safe here in my desk overnight. First thing tomorrow morning I'll take them into town and see if I can find a good photographer who can bring up the details."

Chapter 7

It was almost supper time when Chrissy finally returned looking exhausted and discouraged. But at the sight of the company, she forced a smile.

Mr. Simpson introduced her to Bobbi and Lion.

Was she ever good looking, Lion mused silently. He knew from what Dad had told them earlier that she was thirteen, and unfortunately he was only twelve and a half. But that didn't matter these days, he told himself firmly. Besides, he was almost twelve and three quarters.

"I wish you could meet my son, Todd," Mr. Simpson added."He's sixteen and a great lad. You'd like him. As a rule, he manages to get home for a visit every couple of weeks or so, but lately he's been too busy. He's taking his high school down at the coast because he can't get the art courses he wants at the school here, and there are some special summer courses he's hoping to get into."

"Art school is a pretty expensive business, isn't it?" Dad asked.

Brock Simpson nodded. "But this summer's courses are already paid for, and surely this stupid run of bad luck can't continue."

"Do his instructors think Todd is a good artist?"

"Very." Mr. Simpson's face relaxed into a smile."I'm hoping he'll get it out of his system and come home to learn the ranching business, but you know teenagers. At the moment he's convinced ranching isn't his bag and is determined to prove he can make a life for himself as a struggling artist in the big city. However, he's promised to come home for a good long visit before summer is over."

"I don't care how late in the summer it is, just so long as he comes." Chrissy's voice was soft.

"Is he the lad you used to tell me about who was so good at inventing things?" Dad asked.

Mr. Simpson nodded. "Maybe that goes hand in hand with being an artist. He can invent just about anything." He turned to Chrissy, smiling at her fondly. "Remember all those complicated switches he made for your electric train system, so all four trains could go in different directions at once?" He turned back to Dad. "You'd swear they were sure to crash into each other. But just at the last minute, a switch would be tripped, and each train instead of plowing into another one would suddenly shoot off in another direction."

"I really miss him," Chrissy admitted, her face warm with emotion. "I wish he'd hurry and finish art school, then come back and do his painting from here."

"I wish he would too," Mr. Simpson admitted, smiling. "And I think he will when he's ready. We'll just have to give him time." Then in an altogether different voice he said brightly, "Now why don't you take Lion and Bobbi out and show them around the place while their Dad and

I do something about rustling us all up some supper? They might like to see some of your jumpers. And while you're at the barn, check on Shamrock. That foal of hers could be coming almost any time now."

Chrissy nodded.

Lion had an idea that the real reason Mr. Simpson wanted Chrissy to take Bobbi and him down to the barn was so he could talk to Dad about the trouble he was in. And for a moment he wondered if there was some way he could be allowed to stay. But it was obvious from Dad's expression that he knew exactly what Lion was thinking and was already one jump ahead. Reluctantly, Lion moved after his sister and Chrissy.

He reached the barn just moments after they did. The man Mr. Simpson had introduced as Warren Montcrief was just coming out, still punctuating each stride with the flick of his riding crop against the black leather of his boot.

"Mr. Montcrief owns the ranch across the highway," Chrissy explained, as the stocky, dark-haired figure disappeared. "I don't know what I'd do without him," she added with a grin.

"How d'you mean?"

"He really doesn't know much about cattle and horses. His main interest is financial investment and business development. But he likes the rancher role."

"Which explains the jodhpurs and riding boots," Bobbi put in with a smile.

"Exactly. The real ranchers wear jeans. Actually," Chrissy admitted, "I've never even seen Mr. Montcrief up on a horse, but he enjoys playing the part and since he's got lots of money, he hires a foreman who attends to all the business end of running his ranch and hires me to break and train all his horses." She grinned. "Then he raves to all the other ranchers about the great job I've done, and when they have problem horses, they send them to me for schooling too."

"He said you were going to give his daughters lessons. Do you do much of that?"

"No, but I'd like to," Chrissy's admitted. Her smile broadened. "If I do a good job with Mr. Montcrief's two girls, maybe he'll spread the word and some of the other ranchers will hire me to teach their kids too. It's fun." Her expression sobered. "It's also good money, and right now we can use it." Abruptly she broke off for another newcomer had come into the barn.

He was tall, blond-haired, seventeen or eighteen, Lion decided, with enough resemblance to the man who had just left to suggest he was probably his son. But there the resemblance ended. It wasn't just that this younger edition wore skin tight jeans and a screaming red and yellow shirt instead of neat riding clothes, it was also his lord-of-the-manor walk and his down-the-nose way of studying people.

The moment the newcomer had appeared, Chrissy had edged over against the wall to allow him to pass without coming close to her. At the same time she was pretending to be busy studying a mare in a nearby stall.

The blond-haired teenager swaggered past them

with a smug self-assured smirk on his face and moved on down the barn passageway.

Bobbi waited till he was a good dozen paces away, then said brightly, "So, tell us about your brother Todd."

Immediately Chrissy's smile was back. "As Dad told you, he's fun, loves animals and is really good at art. What he likes best is drawing animals in their natural habitat."

"How does he find them to draw?" Lion put in. "Dad said a lot of the animals around here are almost extinct."

"That's true. But Todd watches them from far away with high powered binoculars so he doesn't frighten them."

Chrissy had been too busy talking to notice that the owner of the screaming red and yellow shirt had stopped within easy hearing distance. Now turning back he retorted in a sneering tone, "As if anybody is going to believe that fairy tale! Why d'you think he comes home for a quick visit every couple of weeks or so? To replenish his bank account by doing a little poaching, of course —"

Chrissy spun around. "Get out of this barn and get off our property!" Her voice was shaking with such anger, Lion was amazed she could get the words out at all. "I'm sick of the rumours you're always trying to spread. Go play your vicious games somewhere else."

The smug satisfaction on the newcomer's face increased even more. Without the least hint of embarrassment, he sauntered leisurely back the way he'd come, the lord-of-the-manor walk even more pronounced.

"That's Mr. Montcrief's son," Chrissy said in a tight voice. "I like his dad, but Kurt is useless, unreliable and vicious. I don't know why Dad agreed to hire him to do handyman jobs here on the ranch."

Bobbi had been watching the swaggering figure move away. Now she glanced sharply at Chrissy. "Isn't he any good at fixing things?"

"He's a joke." Chrissy's tone was acid. "And Dad knew that before he hired him. Only Mr. Montcrief was so sure working over here would give Kurt the experience he needed to start taking an interest in ranching, that Dad hated to say no." Chrissy's face softened into a smile. "For weeks he's been supposed to fix the lock on that window in the main floor bedroom where you'll be sleeping, and he still hasn't done it. I hope you're not nervous at night."

Bobbi laughed. "Not the slightest. I like fresh air too much."

Lion was hardly listening. He was still trying to make sense out of Kurt Montcrief's parting remark. Dad had said that the Ministry people suspected that someone on the ranch might be poaching endangered species. Could it be Todd? Certainly Kurt Montcrief had lost no time in accusing him. Or was Kurt the poacher? Had he said that about Todd because he was looking for a fall guy?

Lion's jumbled thoughts returned to Chrissy's brother. If Kurt's implication was true and Todd really was responsible, it would devastate Dad. Having to act against Mr. Simpson's son would be just as bad — or even worse — than having to act against Mr. Simpson himself.

But Todd couldn't be responsible, Lion told himself firmly. If he was anything like Chrissy, there was no way he could …

That thought died uncompleted, for being Chrissy's brother had nothing to do with it. He knew dozens of kids with brothers or sisters entirely different from them. If Todd really was a "struggling artist," then cash could be a problem. If a chance came along to make a little extra, might the temptation be too great? As Dad always insisted, nobody could ever be one hundred percent sure what someone else might do. Ninety-nine percent maybe, but never a hundred.

Firmly, he pulled his thoughts back. He hadn't even met Todd yet, and until he did, he wasn't making any snap decisions one way or the other.

By now both Chrissy and Bobbi had left the barn.

Lion hurried after them. "Why would that guy spread a vicious rumor like that?" he asked, catching up.

"Kurt? Because he hates Todd. He knows Todd stands to inherit the ranch someday, and Kurt would give his left arm to own this place."

"But you said they have their own place."

"They do. But it's not nearly as big. Besides, land doesn't mean *ranching* to either Kurt or his dad. They both picture themselves as country gentlemen. Mr. Montcrief wants to own land because it gives him a life style and a position in the community that he wants, but he's really a developer and promoter with an office in town." Her smile faded and her voice turned cold. "The reason

Kurt wants land is because he sees it as cold, hard cash in his pocket."

"How d'you mean?"

Chrissy was still watching Kurt swagger away across the ranch yard. "I haven't any proof," she admitted. "It's just a feeling I have. But Kurt thinks he's about the smartest wheeler-dealer in North America, and lately he's been even more smug and self-satisfied than usual. In fact, you'd think from the way he's been acting that he's just discovered some brilliant scheme to make himself into an overnight millionaire. The one good thing," Chrissy added, her face relaxing, "is that if Kurt has some scheme, you can bet it'll be a pretty simple one. He isn't smart enough to dream up anything complicated."

Lion felt himself go cold inside. What if Kurt was planning to get rich by doing exactly what he was hinting that Todd might be doing — poaching and selling endangered species! He'd make piles of money, with very little risk — particularly if he poached those endangered species off the next door neighbour's land instead of his own and had already carefully planted the idea that it was Todd who was behind it!

Another thought struck, and the empty feeling inside grew larger. Could one reason why Kurt disliked Todd so much be because he was afraid that at any moment Todd might hit on that same plan for getting rich and beat Kurt to it?

Chapter 8

As soon as dinner was over, Dad and Mr. Simpson announced they'd done their duty as chefs and were going for a walk, and that Chrissy, Bobbi and Lion could do the clearing up. For the first few minutes they worked in silence, then Chrissy said unexpectedly, "Of course, there's another reason why Kurt hates Todd."

Startled, Lion looked over. Had Chrissy guessed what he'd been thinking earlier? Could she read his mind the way Bobbi could?

"Kurt's jealous because Todd is so smart about inventing things," Chrissy continued.

Lion relaxed. She hadn't guessed his thoughts after all.

"I wish you could see all the games he used to make for me when I was little." As Chrissy talked the anger drained from her face and was replaced by a soft look of pride. "Time locks were his specialty, like the timing switches for our electric train set that Dad told you about and the time locks he put on all the barn doors." She started to smile. "The lock on each stall was set for a different time, starting shortly after dawn, so the doors would open one at a time and the horses would head calmly out at their own pace instead of stampeding and maybe hurting each other. And while they were all casually wandering outside when they felt like it, Todd and I were happily asleep in bed.

Both Bobbi and Lion laughed.

"But the best thing Todd made was Break Away." A far-away look came into Chrissy's eyes.

"Break Away?"

"A galloping horse carved out of dark mahogany that he made for me for my tenth birthday. His head was high and his eyes were bright with excitement and his mane and tail were flying. That's why we named him Break Away." It was as if Chrissy was seeing the little mahogany horse right there. "He wasn't just a horse, he was also a wind up alarm clock with the works hidden inside and the clock face and hands showing on one of his sleek sides. I kept him on my bedside table. Every night before I went to sleep, I set the clock alarm on his side to tell me when it was time to get up in the morning, then wished him goodnight."

"Is he still on your bedside table?" Bobbi asked, scraping the last of the plates and preparing to add it to the rest of the dirty dishes.

Embarrassed, Chrissy shook her head. "He was until last Christmas. Then Dad said I either had to tidy up my room and get rid of some of the stuff or move to a bigger one, so I took all my childhood toys and trains and games and put them away safely in the toy cupboard in the basement. I wasn't going to put Break Away with them. I was going to keep him in my room. But

Todd said he'd be lonely if he was the only one left upstairs—that he'd want to go with the rest of his friends. So, he made a special stable on the top shelf of the toy cupboard where Break Away could be with everyone else but in a place of honour so he'd know how special he was. Then Todd put a lock on the toy cupboard door so he'd be safe and nobody could take him out and damage him."

"Can we see him?"

"Of course. Just let me put in the detergent and turn this thing on, then I'll get the key."

But just as Chrissy was about to take them downstairs to the basement to see the toy horse, Mr. Simpson and Dad arrived back from their walk. "Did you settle those times with Montcrief?" Mr. Simpson asked, coming into the hall.

Chrissy gave him a puzzled look. "Times for what? I saw him briefly leaving the barn this afternoon, but he didn't stop to talk. And I haven't seen him since."

"That's odd. We met him a little while ago when we were walking. He said he was on his way here." He glanced out the window. "I wonder where he could have got to. Never mind. It was about those jumping lessons for his girls. He seems really concerned about getting them settled. Perhaps you should phone him."

Chrissy nodded. She gave Lion and Bobbi a resigned look. "Settling times with Mr. Montcrief can take a while, so you two go ahead. Don't wait." She held out the key. "Introduce yourselves to Break Away. He's in the special stall on the top shelf of the toy cupboard. You can't miss him." With that she turned and went to the phone.

Brock Simpson and Dad had disappeared into the living room to catch the news on TV, and Lion and Bobbi started down the stairs to the basement.

It was only a little after eight o'clock, but already the large basement room was deep in shadows. "What did she mean we can't miss him?" Lion complained, struggling to make out anything at all in the semidarkness. The only light seemed to be a small forty-watt bulb hanging high up at the ceiling. "If I'd known it was going to be this dark, I'd have brought a flash light."

"Stop complaining," Bobbi told him, moving toward the far wall. "The toy cupboard must be over there." She moved in the direction she was pointing. "Yes, here it is." For a moment she struggled unsuccessfully in the half darkness trying to fit the key Chrissy had given them into the lock on the cupboard door. Finally she succeeded in getting it open. At the same moment footsteps sounded behind them.

"Good, here's Chrissy now." Bobbi sounded relieved. "I'm glad you came down, Chrissy," she called turning back to face the stairway. "In the dim light I wasn't sure we'd be able to find Break Away, even with your directions."

There was no answer, only a sudden shifting of the shadows behind them.

Lion could feel the prickles starting to run across his shoulders. He held his breath and listened. Somebody was down there, he was sure of it — he could feel someone watching — someone who was deliberately trying to blend in with the shadows.

He'd had enough. "Come on. Let's get the toy horse and go back upstairs, okay?" he told his sister in what he hoped sounded like his voice. Moving up beside the toy cupboard he began feeling around in the semi-darkness for the horse. At last his fingers closed around it. The polished wood felt smooth and warm under his fingers."I've got it, so let's go, okay?" Without waiting for an answer he started back toward the stairs leading back up to the comfortably light upper hall. But with every step the prickles grew stronger, because he knew they were still being watched. In fact, he could hear stealthy breathing. What if whoever it was decided to jump him from behind?

He'd reached the bottom of the stairs. With a feeling of relief, he was about to start up at a run, when he remembered Bobbi. Forcing himself to stop and turn back, he searched the darkness. Was that Bobbi over there? He couldn't be sure. But he didn't want to have to go back across that basement to see. "Are you okay?" he called in what he hoped she'd think was a normal voice.

In the next second he felt someone or something move past him. "Bobbi?" he managed, this time in a voice that didn't even resemble his.

"Mmm hmmm," a tight voice came back to him from half a dozen steps above.

Through his fear, Lion felt himself grinning. He didn't know who was down in the basement or what they'd come down for, but at least he wasn't going to have to face an evening of teasing at the hands of his sister. She was just as scared as he was!

"So did you get Break Away?" Chrissy called, coming out of the study as they reached the top of the stairs.

For a moment neither of them could trust themselves to answer. Then Bobbi managed a "yes." But to Lion's delight it sounded tight and funny and she was breathing just as rapidly as he was.

"Could you see all right?" Chrissy went on. "I should have given you a flashlight. I keep forgetting that other people don't know their way around in our gloomy basement."

"It was fine," Bobbi managed, recovering her self-control as she talked. "Only it was pretty dark, so instead of just looking at Break Away in the cupboard, we brought him up." As she spoke she reached over and took the horse from Lion. "I hope you don't mind. We can take him back down again in a few minutes if you like."

Lion threw her a dismayed look. Maybe she was eager to go back down into that basement, but he sure wasn't. Not even if Chrissy did want Break Away put back down.

"No, don't take him back." Chrissy moved closer and gazed affectionately at the gleaming mahogany toy. "I think he gets lonely down there. Let him stay up with you for the night. He'd like that." Her eyes softened as she continued to look at the horse. "Isn't he beautiful?"

Bobbi nodded.

Lion knew she was avoiding his eyes, and it was all he could do not to grin, for he knew his sister had been no more eager to go back down that basement than he had. He wondered what excuse she'd have come up with if Chrissy had said that Break Away did have to go back down.

"I still haven't arranged that lesson schedule," Chrissy went on, "because Mr. Montcrief isn't in. He told Dad he was coming here, but he must have changed his mind. He's out somewhere, because there's no answer on his phone, which means I'll have to keep trying." She gave them a resigned smile. "I guess that means I'll see you guys in the morning." With another smile she went back into the study.

"As if you were going to go back down to the basement even if she'd asked you to," Lion teased as Chrissy disappeared. "Why didn't you say anything to her about somebody being down there?"

"Why didn't you?" Bobbi countered, starting toward the room that was to be hers for the visit.

"I was afraid she'd think I was being a sissy," Lion admitted with an embarrassed grin. He wasn't about to spell it out, but he had an idea the way to impress a girl who was already half a year older wasn't by admitting he was scared of the dark.

Chapter 9

Lion wasn't sure if he'd been asleep or not, but suddenly a sound in the hall just outside his door drove all thought of sleep from his mind. There was no mistaking what that sound was — stealthy footsteps.

Holding his breath, he strained to listen. Ordinary footsteps never seemed to catch anyone's attention, but slow, creeping, stealthy ones were something else. What could they mean?

He was still lying motionless, trying to decide whether or not he should get up and check when he heard a door opening stealthily then *snuck*-ing quietly closed.

Instantly he was out of bed, moving on soundless bare feet towards his own door. He eased it open — just in time to see his sister's door handle stop turning.

For a moment he was so surprised he didn't even move. He just stared at the closed door. Had it been Bobbi he'd heard? But why would she be tiptoeing around the house in the middle of the night? He'd better go and find out, he decided. Crossing the hall, he pushed open Bobbi's door without bothering to knock. "Is something wrong? Why are you —?"

Pulling him into the room, Bobbi closed the door then asked in a whisper, "Did you see anyone in the hall a minute ago?"

"You may find this hard to believe," he told her at his driest, "but since it's the middle of the night, I was asleep. At least I was till you went creeping by my door and woke me up. What's going on?"

"That's just what I'm wondering, because it wasn't me. I was asleep too — till I heard those same footsteps." She sat down on the edge of her bed. "Are you sure you didn't see anybody as you came out of your room?"

"Positive."

"But how could a person vanish in the few seconds it would have taken you to open your door and look out? People don't just disappear."

"That girl from the pasture does," Lion told her teasingly.

"Don't be dumb."

Lion's bare feet were freezing on the wood floor. He rubbed first one on the opposite pyjama leg and then the other, but it didn't help. "Let's talk about it tomorrow, okay? I'm going to go back to —"

"Look!" Bobbi pointed across the room. "Maybe it *was* that girl!"

Lion looked where she was pointing. The bedroom window was wide open and the curtains were blowing in the night breeze. "Come on, Bobbi," he told her disgustedly. "Just because the wind blows, it doesn't mean that girl is causing it. In case nobody has ever told you, there's such a thing as hot air rising and cold air rushing in to take its place."

Bobbi grinned. "I didn't know you were such an authority. You must have been paying attention in science class after all." Her glance returned to the window. "But maybe that's why you didn't see anybody in the hallway. Maybe the person we heard tiptoeing around used my window for a get away."

"You mean you didn't open it?"

Bobbi shook her head. "When I went to bed the wind was blowing so hard I decided to leave the window closed for a while and open it later on if the room got too hot."

A frown creased Lion's face. "Then at least that proves one thing: Whoever we heard in the hall can't have been either Mr. Simpson or Chrissy. It must have been somebody who came into the house for some reason, knew how to get in, did what they'd come to do, then left again. Only instead of risking going all the way back to the door, decided to use your window for their exit."

"They must have known Kurt hadn't fixed the lock." For the first time Bobbi sounded uneasy.

"Not if they were using the window just to leave by," Lion pointed out. "Even if Kurt *had* fixed the lock, a person could still open it from inside."

"I suppose. But who would be coming into Mr. Simpson's house in the middle of the night?"

"I don't know. But let's talk about it in the morning, okay? My feet are freezing." Not giving his sister a

63

chance to say anything more, Lion headed back to his own room and to bed.

But not to sleep. He hadn't let on to Bobbi, but he didn't like the idea of somebody from outside coming into the house and using her window. Tomorrow, he'd tell Dad.

He kept thinking about all those weird accidents Mr. Simpson had told them about, particularly the one to poor Epic. It was just luck that Chrissy had been worried because of the wind and decided to ride out and check —

A funny feeling settled somewhere deep in his middle. He'd just finished reminding his sister that just because the wind blew it didn't mean that girl was around, but what if she might be? She'd been here yesterday. When he and Bobbi had been waiting for Dad they'd seen her climbing the hill toward the field where Epic had been pastured. What if she'd sensed the horse was in trouble and deliberately started up that wind so Chrissy would go check? The time would be just about exactly right …

Firmly, he pushed the thought away. Next thing he'd be believing that girl really was somebody different.

But he was a long time falling asleep.

Chapter 10

Next morning Lion arrived at the breakfast table a few minutes after Bobbi. They were the last. Everyone else must have finished earlier, for their places were cleaned away.

He'd been intending to ask Bobbi if she thought there could be any connection between Epic's accident and the gusty wind and that girl they'd seen climbing toward the pasture, but one look at her drawn face made him change his mind. Obviously she had enough to worry about. So, instead, he reached for the cereal box and announced matter-of-factly, "I'm starved."

Bobbi continued to stare at the untouched piece of toast in front of her.

Was she worrying about the same thing anyway, he wondered? Deliberately keeping his voice casual he asked, "What's up?"

Bobbi forced a smile. "Which do you want first? The good or the bad?"

"The bad." She couldn't have been thinking about the girl and the wind after all, he realized with relief.

Bobbi took a deep breath. "Those bank ID pictures are missing from Mr. Simpson's desk drawer."

The relief evaporated. "How d'you know?"

"Chrissy told me. She was still having breakfast when I came to get mine. She said her dad was really upset."

Lion could believe that. "Maybe they've just been moved."

Bobbi shook her head. "The drawer has been rifled through as well." She paused, then watching Lion carefully added, "Mr.Simpson thinks it must have happened during the night, because he had been working at his desk just before he went to bed and everything was in order then."

Lion's uneasiness doubled, for the look on his sister's face made it clear she was thinking the same thing he was — that the person who took the ID photos was probably the person who was in the hall last night and left by using Bobbi's window.

The silence stretched out. Lion was frantically trying to think of some way to break it when Bobbi said bluntly, "We've got to tell Dad and Mr. Simpson that somebody was in the house last night."

"Come on! No way! If we tell Dad somebody was in your room, he'll probably decide we're both in deadly danger and ground us inside the ranch house."

"I don't care if he does." Again Bobbi's voice was tight. "It's okay for you — you've got a room with a window that locks. But anybody can come in and out of my window anytime they want."

For the first time Lion realized his sister had a point.

66

"You're right," he admitted. "We'll tell Dad and Mr. Simpson as soon as —"

Running footsteps in the front hall interrupted him. In the next second, Chrissy appeared in the dining-room doorway. "Have you two sleepy heads finished breakfast?" she asked in an excited voice. "Because Shamrock is foaling! Your dad and mine are already down at the barn and they sent me to get you."

"Chrissy, there's something I —" Bobbi began. It was too late. Already Chrissy had turned and was heading back out the door at a run.

Though she still hadn't eaten any breakfast, Bobbi got up from the table and followed.

Lion remained in his chair. He spooned down his milk and Raisin Bran, shoved two pieces of toast into the toaster, smeared them with butter and jam when they popped up, then with one piece in each hand, started after his sister and Chrissy. He'd suddenly remembered that Bobbi hadn't gotten around to saying what the "good" thing was that she had to tell him.

Chapter 11

The foal had arrived by the time Lion reached the barn. He was gorgeous — gangling and wide eyed with legs all out of proportion to his body and a funny tail that looked wispy and too short for his legs. He walked in a wide-legged way as if not sure he was going to stay on his feet, but he knew who his mummy was, and he had no intention of letting her get one inch away from him, even if walking in a straight line was a bit difficult.

Dad, Mr. Simpson, Chrissy and Bobbi were all staring at the colt in fascination, but Lion's attention was on his sister. He wanted to find out if she really was going to tell Dad about last night. For the moment Bobbi was deliberately ignoring him, but at last she looked over. Giving him an unmistakable nod she moved over closer to Dad.

At that same moment, the sound of brisk business-like footsteps sounded in the barn doorway. In the next second, Mr. Montcrief appeared beside them. "I heard about the colt," he said, joining the others outside the large box stall where Shamrock, ears back, was daring any of the onlookers to come too close to her baby. "What are you going to name him?"

Chrissy didn't even look around but continued

admiring the little colt. "Something special. Caesar, maybe, or Thor or Thunderbolt."

"Why not Break Away?" Mr. Montcrief suggested.

Chrissy's face broke into a delighted smile. "Of course! That's the perfect name for him."

With a nod Mr. Montcrief moved on to check his own horses.

Satisfied that the colt was healthy and normal, Mr. Simpson was already moving in the direction of the barn doorway. "Will you come back to the house with me, Syd?" he asked quietly. "I'd like your advice about what we should do."

"About those missing ID shots, I bet," Lion whispered quietly to his sister. He pointed at Dad and Mr. Simpson, who had reached the doorway. "If you really want to tell them about last night, you'd better do it now."

Bobbi nodded. "Can I speak to you for a minute, Dad?" she called, moving forward. "It's fairly important."

At Bobbi's words Dad turned back, but instead of letting her continue he said gently, "Whatever it is will have to wait, honey. I've promised Mr. Simpson I'll attend to some important business with him." His smiled softened. "While we're doing that, why don't you and Lion take those horses of ours for a good run. They spent a long time yesterday in that trailer. They need to stretch their legs. By the time you get back, Brock and I will be through talking business and then you and I can talk for as long as you want." Without waiting for an answer, he turned and, matching steps with Mr. Simpson, moved off toward the house. Bobbi stared after them with a troubled frown.

"Is something wrong?" Chrissy asked from the box-stall doorway where she was still keeping half an eye on the little foal.

"Oh … oh, no … nothing important," Bobbi answered quickly. She turned her attention to the foal too. "Is he Shamrock's first?" she asked in a casual tone.

"Mmm-hmmm. So she hasn't a clue about how to nurse and of course neither has he. This next little while is crucial."

It was true. The mare was struggling to teach the little foal to nuzzle milk, but he kept circling around her with no sense of purpose. Each time she put him into a corner and tried to press against him so he'd smell the milk, he moved up instead to her head.

"I'll give them an hour to get it right," Chrissy said, amusement in her voice, "then if they still haven't managed, I'll take some milk from Shamrock and feed him with a bottle. Otherwise, he could get too tired to nurse at all."

"Do you want us to wait with you," Bobbi asked. "Is there any way we can help?"

Chrissy shook her head. "By the time you get back from your ride, everything will be fine, but I just want to stay around to make sure. Here, I'll show you where to go." Quickly she sketched a rough map on a piece of paper then, moving to the barn doorway, she pointed. "Head straight that way. You can't get lost because the trails lead right into each other. But keep to the road. Don't take the short cut. It goes off our property in one spot and goes over a garbage hill that can get really treacherous some times in the year. There must be hidden holes in it. Sometimes you can see gas bubbling up from all the stuff that was buried there years ago, before people began being concerned about things like that. Sometimes, for no reason at all, the sand can suddenly start to shift and fall away under the horses' feet." She paused, then added, "Actually it's probably safe right now because the weather hasn't been dry, but just the same it's best to stay clear of it."

Lion hardly listened. Going riding was the last thing he wanted to do. And as they started toward the pasture where Raj and Brie were grazing, he muttered darkly, "Why can't the dumb horses exercise themselves? They've got a big, huge pasture to run around in. Why do we have to be involved?"

Bobbi looked over at him grinning. "I almost forgot! Remember I said I had a good thing and a bad one to tell you? Well, when you hear the good thing you'll stop complaining about exercising the horses. Because Chrissy says that crop circle Dad told us about is right here on ranch property at the very top end of the north pasture. She thinks as Dad does, that the whole thing is a prank of some kind, but she's told me how to get there if we want to check it out." She beamed. "So we can do that and exercise the horses at the same time."

Lion hardly waited for her to finish before breaking

into a run. He wished he'd brought his camera, but he wasn't going back for it now. If he did, Dad or Mr. Simpson might ask where he and Bobbi were going, then say that the crop circle was off limits. He'd never forgive himself if he was this close and then blew it!

But though he couldn't take his camera, he would take his lasso, he decided. Who knows, maybe it would be useful.

Ten minutes later as he finished grooming and saddling Raj, he set to work to tie the rope onto the side leathers on his saddle.

"Why do you always have to take that dumb lasso along?" Bobbi asked irritably. "You never use it. In fact, you don't even know how to use it."

"Cowboys always carry lassos," Lion retorted.

Bobbi's eyes lifted briefly skyward, but she didn't say anything more.

At last Lion had the rope firmly tied and was ready. They set out following Chrissy's map.

It was just as Dad had said when they were driving up. Lion couldn't believe how varied and rich the countryside was. One minute they were in open grassland, the next in a quiet wooded area, then a moment later on the bank of a meandering stream. Ordinarily, he'd have wanted to go slowly and explore. But he could explore later. Right now what he was interested in was that crop circle.

"Are you sure you know where it is?" he asked for the dozenth time. "Maybe we've already passed it. Chrissy said the north pasture, but how do we know we haven't passed the north pasture?"

Bobbi was starting to wonder if they'd missed it too, for they'd been riding for almost an hour. She was just about to suggest that maybe they'd better start retracing their steps when, off in the distance, Lion spotted what looked to be a large, sun-baked pond and beside it, protected by a wind break of tall poplar trees, a dilapidated wooden cabin. The door was hanging at a drunken angle and held by just its bottom hinge, for both the middle and upper hinges had broken off. The windows on either side of the front door had at one time been boarded up, but now those boards too were drooping crookedly, held in place by just a few nails, giving the cabin the appearance of a dejected, bedraggled orphan peering out at the world through half-closed eyes.

Lion trotted Raj toward it. It wasn't a crop circle, but a deserted shack was better than nothing.

Half a dozen paces from the entrance, he pulled Raj to a stand and jumped off. "So, wait, okay?" he ordered, dropping the reins on the ground and moving closer to the cabin.

Raj knew the command for ground tying and obediently stood motionless.

Lion had reached the half-open door and was peering inside. "Bobbi! Come here!" he called. Tossed in one corner of the shack lying close against the wall were half a dozen oblong-shaped metal frames of some kind, each attached to a length of heavy metal chain. "What are those?" He pointed.

Bobbi had dismounted at the same time as Lion and now followed him to the cabin door and looked in. Her voice turned tight and funny. "Leg-hold traps," she said tersely. "For trapping animals. They're cruel and horrible. People aren't supposed to be allowed to use them anymore — at least not unless they are the new kind that have off-set jaws or thick padding around both jaws so when they snap shut they don't break the bone. But even the new ones are still cruel and awful, for the poor animals are so terrified at being caught by one leg that they sometimes chew that leg off in order to escape and then of course die from shock and loss of blood."

Lion felt sick thinking about it.

"The one good thing," Bobbi went on, still staring at the pile of cruel traps, "is that those ones look so old and rusty that they've probably been here for years. They probably don't even work any more."

"Let's take them out and bury them just in case, so nobody can even try to use them," Lion suggested. He was just about to step over the crookedly hanging door when the same prickly sensation that he'd felt last night in the basement started rippling across his shoulders. Quickly, he looked around — just in time to see movement behind a clump of bushes off to his right.

"Don't turn around, Bobbi," he said in a low undertone, "but somebody's watching us."

Bobbi drew in her breath sharply but resisted the impulse to turn. "Can you see who it is?"

"No. But someone's standing behind that clump of

bushes."

"But why would they be watching us?"

"Maybe they saw us staring at those leg-hold traps."

Again Bobbi drew in her breath sharply. "Say something casual," she breathed in a whisper.

For a second Lion's mind went blank — then it started functioning again. "This was a dumb place to come riding," he said in a clear voice assuming his most bored tone. "Who's interested in poking around a ramshackle old cabin that's filled with useless scrap iron? Come on, let's go home."

"You're right," Bobbi replied matching his tone. As she spoke she turned back to Brie, checked the girth to make sure it was tight, then swung back into the saddle.

Next moment both of them were riding away.

More than anything Lion wanted to glance back to see if they were still being watched, but he forced himself to act as if he had no interest in anything except getting back to the ranch house.

They continued to ride in what they hoped looked like bored silence for several hundred metres. Deciding they were safely out of sight of whoever had been staring at them, Lion returned to grumbling. "We must have missed the crop circle. Maybe we should go back to the ranch and come back when Chrissy can come with us. We're never going to find it by ourselves.

"Let's try a little longer," Bobbi returned. "We must be going in the right direction because there's the short cut Chrissy was talking about." She pointed to a narrow path branching off from the main trail. "Too bad we can't take it if it really is a lot shorter, but Chrissy said not to."

"Let's take it anyway," Lion protested. "She said it was probably safe enough right now because the weather hasn't been too dry."

"I dunno —"

"Well, somebody thinks it's okay, " Lion said, pointing to a figure a hundred metres ahead of them on the trail. It was impossible to tell from that distance whether it was a man or a woman. "It can't be that dangerous if someone else is taking it," he insisted.

"I guess," Bobbi conceded.

Lion didn't give her a chance to chance her mind. Moving Raj past Brie, he started along the narrow path at a brisk trot.

Bobbi followed.

There was no longer any sign of the figure ahead. They seemed to be the only ones taking the short cut after all. But Lion decided not to mention that to his sister.

They crossed a meadow deep in cornflowers, circled a cattle pond, then continued to follow the path as it wound upwards and cut across the face of a dry sandy hill. Next second the trail had disappeared and the sand under the horses' hooves began shifting.

"Lion! We've got to go back!" Bobbi cried. "This must be what Chrissy meant about the sand falling away beneath the horses' feet!"

It was too late. Both horses were floundering, and both were frightened. Already they were sinking below their

76

hoofs, and with every step more loose sand was shifting under their weight. Lion and Bobbi struggled to turn them back the way they'd come, but the frightened horses fought to keep going in the direction they were headed.

"Lion, we've got to make them turn back!" Bobbi cried in what was near to panic. We can't let them keep going —"

"No!" a firm voice sounded from somewhere above them. "Don't try to turn! If you do the horses will sink in deeper. You must keep going!" The words were half smothered by a wind that had suddenly come up and by the laboured breathing of the horses.

The authority in the voice was reassuring. Instinctively Lion and Bobbi obeyed. Rather than trying to turn the horses, they urged them forward. But the slope got steeper. At one spot both Raj and Brie lost their footing. As they struggled to regain their balance the whole unstable slope began to move underneath them.

Lion was terrified. He glanced at Bobbi to discover that she looked terrified too.

Should they have ignored that voice? Should they have turned back after all?

Just as he was sure it had been a mistake and that they'd never make it across that treacherous sand hill, he felt Raj's front hoofs settle on something firm. A second later the big horse thrust himself out of the knee-deep, loose sand and onto level ground. Seconds later Brie and Bobbi had clambered up and were standing beside them.

For a moment both horses stood trembling with

exhaustion, unable to do anything but struggle for breath. Then Raj gave a mighty shake, snorted through his nostrils — as if to say if that was the kind of ride Lion wanted to take, he could go alone next time — and turned his attention to trying to find some scrap of grass in the dry soil.

Bobbi, however, had turned around in the saddle and was scanning the landscape. "Can you see her, Lion? Where has she gone?"

There was no one anywhere in sight.

Lion had had enough. "I don't understand any of what's going on," he grumbled irritably. "But the one thing I do know is that I'm going back to the ranch."

The tight lines around Bobbi's mouth relaxed into a grin. "Good. And when you decide which trail we should take to get there, I'll go with you."

His sister had a point, Lion realized. With the twisting, turning short cut and then their struggle to get out of that sand, he wasn't too sure even in which direction the ranch house lay. But it had to be somewhere more or less straight ahead, he decided. "Let's try that way," he said, pointing toward a heavily grassed meadow off in the distance.

"At least it isn't sand," Bobbi agreed, grinning. "And if we end up spending the rest of the summer there, at least the horses should have something to eat."

In spite of himself, Lion laughed.

They headed for the meadow in the distance, winding their way first through a thick clump of trees, then threading through boulders so tall it was impossible to see over them. At last they emerged into an open meadow.

Pulling their horses to an abrupt halt, they stared in amazement.

"Look!" Bobbi exclaimed in a breathless voice. "Then this must be the north pasture!" She pointed.

The meadow was covered in thick, undisturbed, knee-high green grass, except for a large spot in the centre where an intricate pattern had been made. First, there was a large, perfectly formed, outer circle. Inside it lay three smaller, concentric circles, each intersected by a series of perfectly matching diagonal lines. And at the very centre was a perfectly formed six-sided star.

But the startling thing wasn't just the pattern. It was that the blades of grass making that pattern hadn't been trampled or broken down. Instead they had been bent over at a height of about four inches from the ground. Not a single blade showed any sign of withering or dying. Each one was still just as green and healthy looking as the untouched grass outside the circle. The only difference was that the grass in the pattern was growing sideways now instead of straight up and down.

Lion was the first to come back to life. He glanced over at his sister, coughed, then in his best twelve-and-three-quarter-voice said matter-of-factly, "It's not real, you know."

Bobbi didn't even seem to hear. She continued to stare in fascination at the pattern in front of them.

"The scientists who have really looked into these things," Lion continued gaining confidence, "admit that there have been a few cases where they really believed the crop circles had been made by some kind of air vehicle, but in those cases there was always a high concentration of electricity around the pattern. There can't be any build-up of electricity around here, or the horses would be freaking out." He nodded at Brie and Raj, who were still recovering from their ordeal on the sand hill and were snatching mouthfuls of the lush green grass.

At last Bobbi looked around. "I've read about those reports too," she countered. "But that doesn't prove this circle can't be real because the scientists all agreed that the high concentration of electricity wouldn't last. They said after fifteen or twenty minutes it would start to dissipate, and after a couple of days it would have completely disappeared. According to Dad, this crop circle has been here for a week."

For a minute Lion struggled to recover from what he had thought was a foolproof argument. "I still say it's not real," he repeated." The chance of there ever having been any electricity here at all is about one in ten million. I bet Dad's right and some of the Okanagan University College grads made this as a con."

Bobbi gave him a scathing glance, but she didn't argue. Instead she gazed thoughtfully back at the pattern pressed into the deep grass in front of them, then said in a funny, thoughtful voice, "I wonder if the person we saw on the short cut was on her way to or from this crop circle."

Chapter 12

By the time Bobbi and Lion got back from the pasture, unsaddled the horses, rubbed them down and left them to graze, Lion no longer even cared about crop circles. He was sore, tired and irritable, and all he could think about was a huge peanut butter and lettuce sandwich and an uninterrupted afternoon of TV watching.

But as they approached the barn, Chrissy was standing in the doorway, frowning at a red sports car coming down the drive toward them.

Seeing Lion and Bobbi, she gave them a sheepish grin. "I'm feeling guilty," she admitted. She nodded at the car. "I have been ever since Shamrock's little foal arrived. Lani used to love seeing the newborn animals — until I made life so miserable for her that she moved out." Again she nodded toward the car. "But just as I'm feeling mega guilty because she doesn't come around anymore, here she is!"

"Lani?" Bobbi asked.

"Dad's ex-wife."

"You mean *your* mom has moved out, too?" Lion put in quickly, moving up with sudden interest from where he'd stopped at the far end of the box stall.

Chrissy grinned. "No. Lani is Dad's second wife. She's the one who moved out." Her grin faded and a soft, lonely smile took its place. "Mom was Dad's first wife. She died when I was nine. Later, Dad married Lani, but the marriage didn't last all that long. Partly because Lani wasn't exactly suited to ranch life but mainly because of me." Again guilt crept into Chrissy's mile. "I wanted it to be just Dad and Todd and me." The guilty smile grew broader. "By the time you're eleven, if you're willing to work at it, you can do a pretty good job of making things tough for a second marriage."

"Did Todd feel the same way?"

"No. He and Lani got along really well. In fact, it was Lani who insisted on setting up that trust money for his art training. I was the only troublemaker."

Lion's eyes met Bobbi's over Chrissy's head. It was his turn to look shamefaced. "Don't feel guilty," he told Chrissy. "I did exactly the same thing when we were up in Powell River and I thought Dad was falling for the school principal there."

"Believe him! He did!" Bobbi said firmly, her eyebrows arching noticeably. "Nobody in the whole world could have been more miserable to live with. Particularly after it occurred to my dumb brother that if Dad *did* marry the principal, she'd be the principal at the school he'd have to be going to."

Chrissy laughed delightedly.

The red sports car had reached the end of the drive. It braked to a stop. A blond-haired woman in a brilliant red blazer-coat, slim fitting black trousers and red shoes with three-and-a-half inch stiletto heels eased herself gracefully out from behind the wheel. Painstakingly, she began picking her way on her tottering heels along the uneven ground that stretched from where she had parked to the house some hundred metres away. Her thoughts seemed totally occupied with crossing that distance without coming in contact with anything that resembled mud, water or manure.

"She hasn't been here in ages," Chrissy continued still staring. "I wonder what she's come for?"

Either Mr. Simpson's meeting with Dad was over, or he'd heard the car and come out to see who had arrived, for he was standing in the ranch-house doorway, watching Lani's progress with a smile. "To what do we owe the honour of this delightful and unexpected visit?" he asked as soon as she was close enough, unmistakable amusement in his tone.

Lani was still too busy negotiating the path to answer. But at last she succeeded in reaching the steps with no speck of dirt staining her red sling shoes or her black dress pants. With unmistakable relief she looked up and smiled. "Hello, Brock. I've come to talk business."

Lion almost laughed at the look of surprise on Mr. Simpson's face. "You've what? In the three years you lived here you said business bored you, and that you didn't wish to be bothered with any of it."

Lani gave him her warmest smile. "True. But I've decided it's my duty to you and to the children to take

83

an interest. It isn't fair of me to leave all the difficult decision making to you. After all, I am a share holder." Not waiting for an answer, she moved past him through the doorway. "Are the ledgers and books and everything still in your study where they used to be?"

In what appeared to Lion to be still a state of numbed disbelief, Mr. Simpson followed his ex-wife into the hall and toward the door of the study.

"This has got to be a joke," Chrissy whispered to Bobbi and Lion as they too moved into the hall. "Lani has never taken the slightest interest in ledgers or account books or annual meetings or anything else. In fact, I don't think she knows even yet that there's any difference between a cow and a heifer.

Lion laughed.

"Shhhh," Bobbi told him.

"Will you explain things to me Brock? You know — financial statements, income, expenditure — that sort of thing."

"When did you start being interested in financial statements?" Brock Simpson still sounded amused.

Lani seemed suddenly self-conscious. Looking away she began fidgeting with the clasp on the shiny, black shoulder bag she was holding in her lap. "Don't laugh at me, Brock. You don't need to tell me anything if you don't want to. But my lawyer thought it would be all right, since I'm a share holder."

The amused look on Mr. Simpson's face changed to one of apology. "Of course it's all right. You can see anything you want to. And I'll explain any of the business details you're not clear on. I just hadn't thought you had any interest in that sort of thing."

Chrissy backed away from the open doorway. "If they're talking business, I'm going back to the barn. I was so busy this morning with the foal that I've neglected Mr. Montcrief's horses. He wants his daughters to start riding tomorrow, so I'd better put them over some jumps for a bit." She turned to Bobbi. "D'you want to come and help?"

"Yes," Bobbi answered immediately. "Then, when we're through, I'm going to find either your dad or mine and get something done about my bedroom window." She threw a quick glance at Lion.

"Has Kurt still not fixed it?" Chrissy asked in a disgusted voice as they moved away.

Lion returned his attention to the study.

"Actually," Lani was saying, "I haven't been interested in any of this until just recently. But now there are some things that I need to … or at least that I'm supposed to be able to …" The rest tailed off.

Was Lion ever glad he'd stayed. He even forgot about that peanut butter sandwich and watching television. Something was up. The question was, what? He waited for Mr. Simpson to ask.

Instead, Brock Simpson took a large, brown ledger-book out of the desk drawer and set it on the desk where he and Lani could both see it. "Let me show you. This looks complicated, but the only important page for our purposes is this final one, the 'Annual Financial

Statement.' First, Expenditures, next Income, then, at the bottom, what accountants like to call Total Assets."

"That's what I was to look for!" Lani exclaimed with unmistakable relief. "Does that mean how much the ranch is worth?"

Lion felt a funny nudge of uneasiness at the back of his mind. Could that be the reason for this visit? Had somebody sent Lani to find out how much the ranch was worth? But if so, who? Again he waited for Mr. Simpson to ask.

But Mr. Simpson hadn't seemed to have noticed anything unusual. In the same helpful tone he continued, "Yes. Total assets means what the ranch is worth with everything included. But there is no guarantee that it would draw that much on the market. It would depend on what the demand was at that particular moment for agricultural property."

Lani continued to peer at the sheet in front of her. "Do I still own forty-eight percent of the shares?"

Mr. Simpson nodded. "You'll remember we set it up that way so I'd have decision making powers without having to bother you about business details. But you can't go ahead on your own and sell any of them. There's something they call the Agricultural Land Reserve."

"What does that mean?"

"An entire ranching property can be put on the market if the conditions of the sale suit the requirements of the Land Reserve Commission. But an owner can't break off pieces and sell them separately without government permission."

"Not even a few acres?"

Instantly Mr. Simpson's face was concerned. "Do you need to, Lani?" he asked quickly. "Do you need money for something? Because if you do, tell me. The one person you could sell a few shares to would be to an other shareholder in the company, namely me. Things are a little tight for us just now because we've had a run of odd accidents, but if you need money, I'll arrange something."

A warm smile came over Lani's face. Leaning forward in her chair, she put her hand over one of Mr. Simpson's. "Thank you, Brock," she told him gratefully. "I'm not hard up, and I don't need to sell. But it means a great deal to know that if I ever am in a spot and need help, I can come to you."

Her hand continued to rest over his. "I wish we'd met three or four years later than we did," she added in the same soft tone. "Or that I'd had the wisdom to realize that your children needed time to accept me. I think we could have had a good marriage if I'd just been a little smarter."

Lion realized with a start that Brock Simpson was off balance. His hand had turned under Lani's and now his fingers were firmly gripping hers. Could he still be in love with her?

For a minute longer Lani continued to smile at him, then she eased her hand free and got to her feet."But if one can't undo the past, one must make the best of it," she said philosophically. "As you know, I'm really not suited to living alone, so I'm considering changing that.

Perhaps before too much longer I may have some interesting news to tell you." She started toward the door.

Mr. Simpson looked genuinely pleased. "A new interest in your life?"

Lani smiled back at him. "I hope so."

"Am I allowed to ask who the lucky man is going to be?"

Lani shook her head, laughing. "That might jinx things. So far it's still just a maybe. However, if it does work out, you'll be the first to know. Now, I really have to go."

Turning, Lani again started across the office toward the hall, and this time she didn't turn back.

Quickly Lion backed out of the doorway, crossed to the kitchen and slipped out the back door. His intention was to get out of sight before anyone realized he'd been listening. But as he reached the trees, he stopped. Mr. Montcrief was coming out of the barn. As Lani saw him, a pleased smile came over her face. But instead of smiling back, Mr. Montcrief looked startled and somehow displeased. In the next second, he'd spun on his heel and disappeared back into the barn.

Lion was puzzled. If Lani had lived here for three years, she and Mr. Montcrief must know each other. Why wouldn't he have gone over and said hello? Why had he looked so ill-at-ease?

But it was none of his business, Lion told himself. And putting the whole thing out of his mind, he headed back to the kitchen for that peanut butter sandwich.

Chapter 13

Sandwich in hand, Lion headed for the barn to join his sister and Chrissy. They were in the ring, each of them mounted on one of Mr. Simpson's new jumpers. Lion had just stopped to watch them putting the young horses over a series of easy jumps, when another vehicle came down the drive and pulled into the ranch yard. This time it was a well-used, red half-ton. Someone in crumpled jeans unfolded himself from behind the wheel and started toward the ring. "I see you haven't lost your form, Chris," he called with a lazy smile.

"Toddy!" Chrissy squealed. Slowing the jumper she was riding to a halt, she jumped down from the saddle. "Toddy!" Next moment she'd handed her horse's reins to Bobbi and was hugging her brother. "I thought you weren't coming till the end of the summer! Did you just get here? Have you seen Dad yet? How was the trip? How long can you stay?"

Todd didn't even attempt to answer the flood of questions. He just grinned and gave his sister another hug, then glanced with friendly curiosity at Lion and Bobbi. "Hi, I'm Chris's brother, Todd," he said.

Quickly, Chrissy made the introductions, then returned to her flood of questions.

As Todd struggled to answer them all, Lion studied him. After the raving build-up Chrissy had given them about her fantastic big brother, Lion had been more than half expecting the guy to turn out to be a nerd, or a swelledhead. But he was neither. To Lion's surprise he found himself instinctively liking his open smile and casual, friendly manner.

"... got to stay two weeks, at least," Chrissy was saying. "Last time, when we had to cancel our photo shoot because the weather was so awful, you promised that the next time you came home you'd take me for sure. Remember?"

"I haven't forgotten," Todd told her fondly. "And for the next seven days there are supposed to be just about perfect conditions. Later on tonight I'll put the camera out and run a test to make sure we've picked the best area, then tomorrow or the next night we'll go for an overnight shoot. Word of honor." Todd grinned down at her. "Now I'd better go find Dad and say hello." Leaving the ring, he returned to the truck, leaned into the back and retrieved a worn suitcase and an even more badly worn backpack from which odd shapes were poking out.

"He *is* going to take me!" Chrissy said delightedly, pointing. "That backpack is stuffed with his photography things and his drawing stuff!"

"What do you mean by a photo shoot?" Bobbi asked.

"That's probably not the right name for it, but it's what

90

I call it. Todd takes his long range camera, picks a spot where he knows the animals will be coming to eat or drink and camps out overnight. He uses a timer and a long range lens so he can get good, clear pictures without having to come close enough to scare the animals away."

"What sort of a timer?" Lion asked.

"To take pictures every five minutes till the film runs out, unless he stops it sooner."

"How does he know any animals will come along?"

"He doesn't. But every time he's gone out so far, something has turned up. And sometimes he gets marvelous shots."

"Is he really going to take you with him?" Bobbi asked, her eyes shining. "Hey, what fun."

Chrissy's eyes were dancing.

A few minutes later, Todd reappeared from the ranch house, minus his bag and backpack, and rejoined the others in the barn. "So, what's new around here?" he asked.

"Come. I'll show you," Chrissy told him excitedly. She led the way to Shamrock's box stall. "Meet Break Away," she said, nodding at the new foal.

Instantly, Todd was at the box stall doorway. "What a neat little guy. Are you really going to name him Break Away?" He seemed pleased.

For a moment they stood watching the new colt and his mother. Then Todd's expression changed. "How are things?" he asked "Has that awful, dead sand hill started growing anything yet?"

Chrissy shook her head.

"Not even some weeds or a clump of bunch grass?"

"Nothing."

"You wonder how long it will be before people —" Abruptly he broke off and said instead in a lighter tone, "Never mind. Tell me about things in general? As you've been riding the trails and keeping an eye on the place for Dad, have you noticed anything new or different?"

Suddenly Lion's attention sharpened, for a note had come into Todd's voice that hadn't been there before — as if he wanted to ask something in particular but didn't like to.

Chrissy must have heard it too, but instead of being puzzled she was laughing. "If you're hinting about what I think you are, yes. I've been keeping an eye on the place for Dad and riding around the trails, and, yes, I've seen something new and different — that crop circle."

"That what?" Todd sounded genuinely puzzled.

"How could I miss when it's on our property?" Chrissy went still grinning broadly. "You and your art school friends did a pretty good job."

"What are you talking about? I heard something about a crop circle being found. I guess everybody did because it was in all our papers. But I didn't know it was on our property. And I had nothing to do with it!" The grin came back. "But if my art school friends and I had thought of it, we just might have made one," Todd admitted. "In fact I wish we *had*. It would have been a neat challenge."

Unless Todd was the greatest actor in the world, he hadn't had anything to do with it, Lion decided.

Chrissy wasn't convinced. "Nice try," she said wryly. "If you weren't hinting about that crop circle, then why the questions about checking out the property and riding the trails?"

Todd's smile disappeared. For the first time he looked guilty and more than a little self-conscious. "I was wondering if there'd been any more trouble — you know, accidents. To be honest, I've been feeling kind of guilty staying down in Vancouver doing my art when you've been having problems here on the ranch."

At Todd's words all the excitement drained out of Chrissy's face. "Oh, Todd, I forgot! I was so excited to see you, I forgot! The worst accident of all happened just yesterday. Epic got caught in some barbed wire!"

"But there's no barbed wire anywhere on the ranch!" Todd protested.

"I know. That's what makes it so scary."

"Is he okay?"

Chrissy's face grew even more worried as she told him what had happened and what the vet had said.

"I better put a hold on my art and come home to give you and Dad a hand," Todd said quietly.

"Oh, Toddy, would you? But not if you don't want to," Chrissy added quickly.

Her brother grinned. "I've been thinking I should," he admitted. "I can do my painting and help with the ranch at the same time. Only I can't for a few more weeks." A gleam of excitement came into his eyes. "Because I've just got my first commission for a painting."

"Your what?"

"Commission. A man who owns a big gallery in Vancouver is going to mount a show of early historical scenes. I was telling him about that neat, old prospector's cabin by the cattle pond, and he's offered me two hundred dollars to do a painting for his show. If it sells, then he says he'll take all the ranching scenes I want to send him."

"Toddy! How terrific!" Chrissy told him.

"The old shack is still there isn't it?" A worried note crept into Todd's voice. "Nobody's torn it down or anything?"

"No. It's still there."

"Good. Then how about riding out with me tomorrow so I can look at it."

As they'd been talking a familiar figure in slim-fitting stretch jeans and a red and yellow shirt had came strolling through the barn doorway. "I thought that looked like your beat-up red truck in the yard," said a drawling voice. "So, the big city artist is finally going to get paid for his work, is he?"

"Hello, Kurt," Todd greeted casually.

"When's this momentous sketching to take place? This afternoon or not till tomorrow?"

"Whenever."

"Can ordinary mortals watch?""

"No."

"Too bad." Kurt turned to Chrissy. "Has my dad been around?"

Chrissy shook her head.

"Then I'll wander outside and wait. He told me he was coming." As he spoke he started back out of the barn.

"While you wait, I think we should talk," Todd said moving after him.

"Get lost." The words were almost covered by the ring of Kurt's footsteps on the wooden barn floor.

Todd continued to follow. Now it was his voice that floated back. "... sooner or later ... get caught ..."

"... barking up the wrong tree, Simpson ..."

"... put a stop to it ... one reason why I've come home ..."

"Then don't be surprised if ..."

Lion couldn't hear any more for they'd moved too far away. But he'd heard enough to know that despite what Todd had told his sister, sketching that cabin and taking her on a photo shoot weren't the only reasons behind this visit.

Chapter 14

Again that night, just as Lion was about to drift off to sleep, he heard muffled footsteps passing his door.

Instantly he was awake. Had someone used Bobbi's window again? She'd said she was going to speak to Mr. Simpson about it, but with the excitement of Todd coming home she must have forgotten.

Quietly, Lion got out of bed. He eased open his bedroom door. He could make out a shadowy figure at the end of the hall and was just about to start in pursuit when a sudden shaft of moonlight from the window made it clear that the shadowy figure was Todd.

So much for playing cops and robbers, Lion told himself disgustedly. He knew Todd had been out a while earlier with Chrissy setting up his camera to run some trial, overnight time exposures to make sure they had a good spot for that photo shoot. Obviously, he'd forgotten something and was going back out for it.

But Todd wasn't going back out. He was standing motionless at the top of the stairs leading down to the basement, listening to something.

Lion heard it too. Someone was moving around down there.

Well, this time Todd could check it out, Lion decided. He'd had enough of people hiding in the basement last night. And he was just about to go back to bed when he heard a *snuck* sound coming from below, as if someone had opened the back basement door and pushed it shut again. Obviously, Todd had heard it too, for like a silent shadow he disappeared down the basement stairs in pursuit.

For one guilty moment Lion wondered if he should go too, but almost immediately he consoled himself with the thought that even a top-grade secret agent would think twice about setting off in the dark in his pyjamas over countryside he had never seen before. Particularly when there was almost no moon. Better to stay where he was and watch from the hall window, he told himself, for it looked right out on the yard where Todd and his quarry would be walking.

Relieved to have made that decision, he moved to the window in time to see two vague shapes moving some fifty paces apart across the open ranch yard. Who the first one was he couldn't make out, for he could only see his back, but the second figure was clearly Todd. Then, even as he watched, the figure in front was swallowed up by the shadowy darkness, and a moment later Todd had disappeared too.

Well, whoever went out would have to come back, Lion told himself, settling more comfortably against the window.

Ten minutes dragged by.

Then it occurred to him that this window looked out in the same direction as the one in his room. If he stayed here and watched, anyone coming along the hall would see him. But if he went back to his room and watched from there, no one would know.

However, another long ten minutes at the window in his bedroom brought no sign of anyone returning to the house.

By this time he was frozen. Maybe he should get back in bed for a few minutes — just till he warmed up, he decided. So long as he listened carefully, he'd have no trouble hearing the kitchen door reopen, and when it did he'd get up and find out exactly what was going on.

But if the kitchen door reopened Lion didn't hear it. Within two minutes of crawling back under the covers, he was fast asleep.

Chapter 15

Todd, on the other hand, had never been more keenly wide awake. As he crossed the ranch yard, he was concentrating so intently on the figure ahead of him that it was hard to breathe normally.

He didn't dare break into a run for fear the person ahead would hear, then put off whatever he'd come out to do until he knew he wasn't being followed. And Todd didn't want him to put it off. He wanted to catch him in the act so he'd have proof. That was one of the reasons he'd come home.

He was pretty sure that the person ahead of him was Kurt, and he was also pretty sure that Kurt had come out to set a couple of those hated leg-hold traps down by the pond where the animals came to drink. That's what Todd had been angling to find out when he'd asked Chrissy about riding the trails. He'd wanted to know if she'd seen any sign of traps, but he didn't dare ask right out in case later on she said something when Kurt or his dad were around.

Somebody had been poaching for several months now, and Todd was almost positive it was Kurt. But he needed proof. It was a real break that Kurt had come out tonight. Maybe at last Todd could get that proof.

He continued to walk quietly through the darkness, his attention on the figure ahead. Kurt was slowly pulling ahead of him, but he'd catch up later, Todd told himself, when there was no danger of Kurt noticing him.

The one thing that puzzled him was why Kurt had first made that side trip down their basement. What had been the point? If he was setting leg-hold traps, as Todd was practically positive he was, why not go straight out and set them? Why go snooping around somebody else's basement?

The shadowy figure ahead was entering a thick clump of trees. Todd increased his pace slightly. He'd have liked to run, but he didn't dare. He knew the sudden movement might catch Kurt's attention, and if it did, there was no way he'd go ahead with his plans. Better to be cautious, Todd told himself. No point in giving the game away now.

Seconds later he too had reached the trees. He moved through them to the other side. Now it would be easy to see his quarry, for ahead lay a large clearing and beyond it the cattle pond.

But Kurt was no where in sight.

Todd felt a wave of panic. Where could he have disappeared to? Frantically he gazed around, but there was no sign of movement anywhere. The only thing in sight was the large, silent equipment shed, sitting all by itself in the clearing. If Kurt had come to set traps, he wouldn't be setting them there, Todd realized. The smell of oil and gas around all that heavy machinery would scare any animals away. Even Kurt or Mr. Montcrief would know that! Somehow, Kurt must have managed to get farther ahead of him than he thought and must be already across the clearing and into the trees on the other side.

Todd hurried to follow.

But though he twice circled the clearing, watching and listening for any sign of movement, then cut over to the cattle pond and walked all around it, there was still no sign of anyone anywhere.

Had Kurt known he was being followed? Had he deliberately hidden?

Disgusted with himself, Todd turned and retraced his steps to the ranch.

Chapter 16

Lion hardly realized he'd been asleep when the harsh jangling of the ranch telephone jolted him wide awake again. He struggled to see the luminous dial of his watch in the meager light coming in the window. Four o'clock! Who phoned their friends at four in the morning!

"Yes? What is it?" he heard Brock Simpson say in a surly, half awake voice into the phone in the hallway. There was a pause, then "My God!" Simpson exclaimed. Then to the house at large, shouted, "Fire! Todd! Chrissy! The equipment shed! Gus says everything is going up!" Slamming the phone down, he raced to his room to grab pants, shoes and a jacket.

Already Lion was dressed and in the hall, to discover that Dad and Bobbi were there ahead of him. So was Chrissy. Next moment Todd appeared, a look of numb shock on his face. Wherever he'd gone, he'd obviously come back Lion realized, but there was no time to worry about that now.

"I'll take some of you in the jeep. Todd will take the rest in the ATV," Mr. Simpson directed. As he spoke he led the way outside.

It was a good thing the equipment shed was situated

off by itself, away from any other ranch buildings, for it was just as Mr. Simpson had said. Everything was engulfed in flames. Not only the area where tools, medicines and grain were stored, but also the attached open ended shed where the seeder, the bailer, the heavy duty tractor and several other pieces of large equipment were stored when they weren't in use.

Gus, the weathered barn-foreman, had put all the available hoses into use and was struggling to keep the flames from moving out into the prairie grass and threatening the whole countryside. For a few moments after they got there, Lion had been afraid the fire was going to jump out of control — that it was going to spread right across the prairie. But fortunately a brisk breeze came up blowing in the right direction — pushing the flames away from the open fields and back onto themselves. Then, shortly after six o'clock, the local fire brigade arrived. With the help of the breeze and the steady flow of water from their hoses, they were able to keep the flames from spreading to the surrounding fields, but it was impossible to do anything to check the holocaust of the burning shed itself. Almost all the equipment it contained was gasoline powered, and as the fire spread, one gas tank after another exploded.

By eight o'clock the shed and the machinery it had contained were a mass of smoldering rubble. But at least the fire had not spread to the fields beyond.

Mr. Simpson was close to tears as he thanked the volunteer firemen for coming.

"Now you go git some breakfast," Gus told him in his gravelly voice. "Stan 'n Martin 'n me will keep our hoses goin' just to make sure nothin' starts up again." He nodded toward the ranch hands.

Mr. Simpson hardly seemed to hear. He continued to stare as if mesmerized by the extent of the destruction.

"I'll phone the fire insurance people," Todd said quietly. He looked grey and shaken.

At that Mr. Simpson looked around. "I just hope we've got enough insurance to replace everything," he managed in a dull, shaken voice.

"Fortunately, we don't have to worry about that," Todd told him, coming back to life. "Remember, last fall we decided to up the amount of insurance we'd been carrying before."

"Only because you talked us into it," Chrissy put in gratefully. She turned to her dad, making her voice as positive and cheery sounding as her brother's. "Am I ever glad you didn't listen when Mr. Montcrief tried to convince you that the new premiums would be too high. Am I ever glad you didn't pay any attention."

For a moment the look of stunned shock on Mr. Simpson's face faded and the hint of a smile took its place. "I seldom pay attention to Montcrief when it comes to ranching matters," he said wryly. But as he glanced around at the circle of exhausted faces, scorched hair and soot stained clothes, the smile faded. "Thank you. All of you," he said in an unsteady voice. He turned back to Gus. "Are you sure you can manage —?"

"I'm sure. Go git some breakfast."

Brock Simpson nodded. He moved with Todd toward the ATV, then turned to Dad. "Will you bring the others in the jeep?"

Dad nodded.

As soon as they got back to the house, Todd went to the phone to call the insurance people. Moments later he joined the others at the breakfast table.

"So, what did they say?" Mr. Simpson prodded.

"I just got their emergency line, for the office isn't open yet, but that person said they'd have someone out to look over the fire site first thing tomorrow morning."

"Not till then?" Chrissy protested.

Her brother smiled. "It will take that long before it's cool enough. Some of those big timbers will continue to smolder for hours." He turned back to Mr. Simpson. "Meantime, the man on the phone said we're not to go near the area or touch anything."

"That's ridiculous!" Chrissy protested again. "Why can't we look at it if we want to? After all, it's our property."

Brock Simpson glanced over at Dad as if wanting his input.

"It's just a formality," Dad explained, helping himself to another piece of toast and marmalade. "But it's one you have to observe. One of the conditions of accident insurance is that the company has the right to have its investigators go over the accident site before anyone else goes near it."

Mr. Simpson nodded. He rubbed a hand across his forehead. "I was sure that accident to Epic would have ended our bad luck."

"Tell me exactly about each of the other accidents, okay Dad?" Todd said quietly.

Mr. Simpson looked as if he wanted to ask why, but must have thought better of it. Instead, he nodded. "First, something contaminated one of the cattle ponds. Fortunately, we discovered it before it did much damage, but we lost a couple of young heifers."

"How did you discover it?" Todd put in sharply.

"Chrissy was out on her horse, checking fences. It was a blistering hot day and her horse couldn't wait to get to the pond for a drink. Only when he got there, he backed up and refused to go near it. So we checked and found a high concentration of gasoline had somehow seeped in." Again Mr. Simpson rubbed his head as if it was aching. "Then, somehow a virus attacked a lot of the cattle — it cut badly into our profits at the annual cattle sale because almost every steer was down in weight. And you know about the tractor and the bailer deciding to die on us without any warning. But the worst was the accident to poor Epic."

"Chrissy said you weren't sure yet if he'll be all right."

"That's true. The vet still isn't saying."

For a long moment after that nobody spoke. Suddenly, a car was heard sliding to a stop in the gravel driveway outside. A moment later Mr. Montcrief and Kurt appeared at the door.

For a moment Lion wondered why they hadn't come over long ago. After all, they were neighbours. If neighbours hear shouting and see clouds of smoke and flames lighting the early morning sky, they come over to see if they can help. But then he remembered the time and realized that maybe it wasn't so odd. After all that had happened, it felt as if it should be at least mid afternoon, but actually it was still only eight o'clock. The fire had started at four. Also, the equipment shed was more than a kilometre away from the Montcrief property. If they were sound sleepers, they could easily have slept through everything at that hour of the morning.

Mr. Montcrief and Kurt said how sorry they were, asked if there was any way they could help and made conversation about how nobody expects anything like that to happen. But it was obvious no one was in the mood to talk, so after about fifteen minutes they went away again.

The day dragged on.

By the time dinner was over that evening, everyone was too exhausted to do anything but go to bed.

It wasn't till Lion was falling asleep that he realized he still hadn't found out who Todd had been following last night or why. He'd also forgotten to check with Bobbi about the lock on her window.

Oh well, he told himself. Tomorrow, for sure, he'd do both things.

Chapter 17

As everyone else in the house fell into an exhausted sleep, Todd lay wide awake on his bed, fully dressed except for his shoes. The guilt inside him continued to grow.

At first this morning they'd all been so busy fighting the fire, he'd had no time to think of anything else. But after they'd come back to the ranch, his mind had started working.

Last night all he'd been thinking about was leg-hold traps and getting the proof he needed to put an end to the poaching. He'd been so sure it was Kurt he was following that he didn't even think about who else it might have been or why that person had gone down their basement. But ever since early afternoon, the frightening suspicion had been growing that the person in their basement last night had gone there for the sole purpose of finding something to use to set that fire — something that would throw the blame on Dad and Chrissy.

He had to find out if his suspicion was correct. Whether the insurance adjuster liked it or not, he had to get a look at the fire scene before any proof that might be there had been removed or destroyed.

Again he checked the sky outside his window. The sun had set almost an hour ago. In another few minutes it would be dark, but he'd wait another half an hour to be sure.

Gradually, the minutes passed. At last Todd pushed himself to a setting position and again checked the sky. Some clouds had blown up and were almost hiding the moon. Good.

He laced his trainers, then quietly he opened his bedroom door, tiptoed soundlessly along the hall and down the stairs. In a moment he was letting himself out of the back door. Keeping to the shadows, he crossed the ranch yard, then broke into a run.

Last night he'd been too dumb to make sense of things, but tonight he intended to get some answers.

Chapter 18

Early next morning, as promised, the insurance adjuster arrived.

The others were still at breakfast, except for Todd who hadn't appeared yet.

At first Mr. Simpson seemed relaxed and unconcerned. "It's strictly a formality," he explained when Chrissy questioned him again about why the inspector had come. But after more than an hour had passed and the insurance man was still busy at the fire scene, Mr. Simpson's worry began to increase.

"Where's Todd?" he asked for the third or fourth time. "He can't be sleeping this long. Go ask him to get up and come down, will you Chrissy?"

Moments later Chrissy returned looking even more worried than her father with the word that Todd was not in his room and his bed had not been slept in. "Also," she admitted in a funny, choked voice, "his truck is no longer parked where he left it in the driveway."

It was on the tip of Lion's tongue to tell her that late last night he'd heard a car revving up and heading back out the drive, but he held the words back. Chrissy was looking so hurt and dejected at the thought that her brother really might have taken off with out saying anything to anyone, that he didn't want to add to her worries.

Mid morning the insurance inspector rapped on the front door and came in. He was holding something just out of sight behind his back.

"Good," Mr. Simpson said with obvious relief. "Are you finished? Is everything all right? Can my son and I drive into town and arrange a bank loan on the strength of the insurance, so we can keep the ranch running?"

The inspector seemed off balance. "I … that is … I am required to make my report to the office, first, then one of my supervisors will contact you."

"But surely you can tell me if I can go ahead and arrange a bank loan …"

"I'm afraid I can't say anything."

"Can you at least tell me if you found anything to suggest how the fire could have started?"

The man looked even more uncomfortable. He shook his head.

"Does that mean no, you haven't found anything?" Brock Simpson asked with a smile, "Or no, you can't tell me?"

"I'm sorry, sir," the inspector repeated politely. "You'll have to wait till one of my supervisors phones you."

The smile vanished from Brock Simpson's face. "That's ridiculous." With an effort he restrained his anger. "But I suppose it's not your fault. You're only obeying orders. Will this supervisor phone me today, do you think?"

"Yes, sir. I'll ask him to."

The rest of the morning dragged, particularly because

Brock Simpson was alternately angry and worried at the continued absence of Todd.

"He can't have gone for good," Chrissy said, "for his camera things and drawing pad are still in his room. Besides, he promised he'd take me on a photo shoot, and he always keeps his promises."

At last just before noon the phone rang. Mr. Simpson took it in the study. It was a long time before he returned to the living room, and when he did his face was tight.

"Was it the fire insurance supervisor?" Chrissy asked quickly.

Brock Simpson nodded. "It seems there will be a delay before they authorize payment."

"Why?" Dad put in quickly.

"He tried to pretend he was being cautious because we'd increased the insurance coverage last year. He tried to make it sound as if that was the issue that needed clarification. But I'm almost positive there was something more — something that he was refusing to mention. Meantime, he said the fire site is to be roped off and no one is to interfere with it in any way." It was obvious Mr. Simpson was trying to hide his concern.

"Did you explain that you'll need to order new equipment immediately?" Dad went on.

Brock Simpson nodded. "I asked for some sort of written acknowledgment to take to the bank stating that the insurance will eventually be paid so we can arrange a loan, but it seems they aren't willing to do that yet either."

It was Dad's turn to look worried.

"Don't they realize we've got to replace that equipment," Chrissy protested. "Don't they realize we can't run the ranch without it?" For the dozenth time she looked around. "Why isn't Todd here? He'd know what we should do."

Brock Simpson turned back to Dad, no longer trying to hide the worry from his voice. "D'you think that inspector found something this morning at the fire site that could be causing them to take that stand?"

"I don't know," Dad replied, "but I'd like to find out. Would you object if I gave him a call? He might tell me things that he isn't ready yet to tell you."

"Would you, Syd? I'd be grateful."

The others waited in silence as Dad went into the study to make the call. When he returned, his face was unreadable. "Apparently they have found something that suggests the fire may have been deliberately set."

"That's impossible!" Brock Simpson exploded. "What sort of something?"

"They're not prepared to disclose that yet."

"But it's not fair to keep us in the dark!"

"I told them that very thing," Dad said, a smile creeping into his voice. "But it didn't seem to impress them."

"Did they say how soon they would tell us?"

"Apparently they'll get in touch as soon as they finish their investigations."

"Surely they don't think it was one of us!"

Dad didn't answer.

As the significance of his silence sank in, the lines

around Brock Simpson's mouth tightened. "If it's —"
He coughed to clear the funny note that had come into
his voice and started again. "If it's true that they have
proof the fire was deliberately set, what will that mean
in terms of delaying the payment?"

"Very little, if they find that none of you had anything to do with it. If the fire was caused by someone or
something else, they'll go ahead and pay you the full
face value of the insurance policy. It's only if they find
some suggestion that someone here was involved that
they will continue to hold things up."

It was as if a huge weight had just been lifted from
Brock Simpson's shoulders. "Then, there's no problem,"
he said with a look of overwhelming relief.

"Mind you, there could still be some delay in pro-
cessing things," Dad cautioned.

"That doesn't matter so long as we know the money
will be coming sooner or later." Brock Simpson glanced
at his watch. "It's not quite one o'clock. I think I'll drive
into town before the bank closes and make some pre-
liminary inquiries. I'm sure the bank will give us a loan.
I've known the manager for a long time." He looked
over at Dad. "Would you come with me, Syd? We can
get some lunch while we're there."

"Of course."

"I wish Todd was here so he could come too," Mr.
Simpson said, looking out the window as if expecting to
see Todd arrive at any moment. "I can't understand
where he could have gone to."

Chrissy was looking even more worried than her father.

"Perhaps we'll find he's at the bank ahead of us," Dad suggested.

Immediately Brock Simpson's face brightened.

"If not," Dad went on, "I'm sure he'll have arrived back here by the time we get back."

Two hours later the men returned.

"Was Todd there?" Chrissy asked excitedly. "Did the bank give you the loan?"

Her dad smiled. "No."

Chrissy gazed at him in confusion. "You mean no, Todd wasn't there, or no, the bank didn't agree to give us a loan?"

"No, to both."

"Then why are you looking so happy?"

"I'm not happy about Todd. In fact I'm worried about him. But I'm relieved about the money."

"But you just said the bank didn't give you the loan." Chrissy sounded even more confused.

"They didn't. But I don't mean they refused. They didn't give me a loan, because I didn't ask for one."

"Why not?" Chrissy protested. "How can we replace the equipment without a bank loan?"

While they'd been talking, Mr. Simpson had been leading the way into the living room. He motioned to everybody to sit down, then returned his attention to Chrissy. "I'm glad you asked, because you should know these things. Some day you may have to make these decisions. I didn't ask about arranging a bank loan because

Mr. Montcrief was coming out of the bank just as we were going in, and he offered to lend us the money instead — at half the interest rate the bank would have charged." The smile on Mr. Simpson's face broadened. "It seems he's got lots of money and offered to lend us whatever we need so we don't have to go through the bank."

"Won't that mean the bank is losing your business? Won't they object?"

The smile on Mr. Simpson's face broadened. "On the contrary, I think the bank manager was relieved. He drew up the papers and acted as witness. It's a win-win situation for all of us because Montcrief is lending us the money for six months at just five percent interest instead of the nine and a half the bank would have charged."

Chrissy frowned. "Is six months long enough?"

"If it isn't, Montcrief has promised to extend it."

Chrissy continued to look as if she had more questions, but she must have decided not to ask them.

For a moment there was silence, then Mr. Simpson added, "There's one more thing. It's purely a technicality, but just the same, both you and Todd should know about it. With any kind of loan it's customary for the person borrowing the money to give the lender some kind of collatoral — something of value that the lender can keep if the borrower should default on the loan. Bobbi's dad, the bank manager, Montcrief and I all agreed that in this case a fair collatoral would be three percent of the shares of Willow Creek Ranch."

"You put up shares of the ranch!" Chrissy exclaimed

in protest. "What if —"

"There's absolutely no cause for worry," Mr. Simpson told her quickly. "The bank manager made sure of that. He made it clear that the transfer of that small group of shares was strictly a formality. As soon as the loan is repaid, those shares will be returned. And to make sure there can be no problem, he had Montcrief sign a statement promising not to sell those shares or dispose of them in any way without my written approval."

"So, holding those shares won't give him any say in the running of the ranch?"

"Almost none. After all, it's only three percent, which makes him a very small shareholder. However, he will have a right to ask questions and voice his opinion." Mr. Simpson smiled. "To be honest," he admitted, "I suspect that could be the reason he offered to put up the money. I think he pictures himself as a country gentleman and is looking forward to sitting in on decision making meetings for a big ranching operation like this."

It seemed to Chrissy that her father could be absolutely right, and at last she relaxed. Her thoughts returned to her brother. "When you were in town, did you ask if anybody had seen Todd?"

Mr. Simpson's face clouded. "No. I didn't want to start a lot of rumours. Todd has his own life. Something may have come up that he felt he had to attend to, in which case he wouldn't appreciate my getting everyone talking about him. But if he isn't back by this evening, I'll start making inquires."

Chapter 19

Later that afternoon, the chief insurance supervisor telephoned.

For a long time after Mr. Simpson put down the phone, he remained at his desk. Finally, he joined the others in the living room. "It seems they have made up their mind about the fire," he said in a funny, tight voice. "They suspected from the start that it must have been deliberately set — apparently the burning pattern pointed to that. Now they say they have found the device that was used to start it." He coughed, then added, "At least that answers the question of why Todd took off."

"Todd! What do you mean?"

"The fire was started by a clock — a clock that had been set into a hand-carved mahogany horse."

"Break Away?" Chrissy's voice caught.

Quickly, Lion glanced cross at Bobbi. Was that what the person down the basement had been looking for three nights ago? Only, he and Bobbi got Break Away first and took him upstairs.

"The insurance people seem to think that the person who made that horse clock is responsible for setting the fire," Mr. Simpson went on in the same expressionless voice.

"But that is ridiculous!" Chrissy exploded. "There's no way that Todd —"

"They know all about the time switches he used to make for your toys," Brock Simpson went on as if Chrissy hadn't spoken. "They say he'd have had no difficulty making the detonating device. The fact that he has disappeared — run away if you like — seems to be adding to their conviction that he is the guilty one."

The realization that Break Away had been destroyed must have suddenly sunk in, for Chrissy's eyes filled with tears. "I should never have put him downstairs," she said more to herself than to the others. "I should have kept him in my room where he'd have been safe." Roughly, she brushed at the tears, and forcing her feelings back declared in a firmer voice, "But if Break Away was used, it proves Todd had nothing to do with it. He'd never have destroyed Break Away! He loved him just as I did! That's why he made him that special stable in the toy cupboard! Besides, he'd have known if he used him it would immediately point suspicion in his direction."

"I tried to point that out," Mr. Simpson said quietly. "They say he would have expected the wooden horse to be completely destroyed, so no one would have known it had been used. And under ordinary circumstances it would have been, only by some fluke the weight of the wire attached to the hour hand rocked the little horse far enough away from the flames that, though it was badly charred, it was still recognizable. They say Todd wouldn't have expected that."

For a long moment, there was shocked silence. Then Chrissy asked numbly, "How could a toy clock start a fire?"

"Simple," Brock Simpson replied, as if talking kept him from thinking or feeling. "Any kind of windup alarm clock will do. You simply take a length of plastic coated or rubber coated wire and glue it to one of the hands of the clock. It's best to use the hour hand, for it's wider as a rule and stronger. You let the wire extend out beyond the end of the clock hand so that it extends over the clock face where the numbers are, then scrape the plastic or rubber off the last inch or so of the wire leaving it bare. Then, you attach the other end of that piece of wire to a battery that has a metal stud at the end."

Lion, Bobbi, Chrissy and Dad were listening intently.

"Then, it's a question of taking two more pieces of wire," Mr. Simpson went on in the same almost numbed tone. "You fasten one from the other end of the battery to your detonating device, in this case a hot plate. The other piece of wire is then fastened from the hot plate back to the clock but not to the hour hand. It is fastened to the clock face itself, beside whatever hour number you have decided to select. It is not lying flat but is left sticking out at right angles to the clock face.

"As the minute hand moves around, it doesn't activate anything because it doesn't stick out far enough to touch anything. But the hour hand has that long piece of wire glued to it, and it sticks out beyond the edge of the clock face. When it reaches the hour where that other piece of wire has been glued at right angles, it completes the circuit and presto, the hot plate turns on."

"Did they know about the hot plate right away?" Dad asked quietly.

Mr. Simpson nodded. "Since it was made of iron, it was of course not destroyed by the fire. But they don't consider it significant, because anybody could have brought a hot plate into the equipment shed. But they're convinced no one except family would know about Break Away."

Suddenly, Lion was remembering something. It wasn't only family who knew about Break Away. Mr. Montcrief knew. He'd been the one who had suggested that name for Shamrock's foal. And if Mr. Montcrief knew, then Kurt probably knew too.

"But how could the hot plate start the fire?" Chrissy's voice recalled Lion's thoughts.

"The insurance man says he expects it had been covered with a thick layer of shavings and grease and probably some gasoline," Mr. Simpson replied. "Once the circuit had been completed, it would take just a few moments for the plate to heat up, then the gasoline would ignite and the whole thing would burst into flames."

For a long moment there was silence.

It was broken by the telephone.

"Maybe that's Todd!" Chrissy exclaimed running to answer it. But when she returned a moment later the

121

excitement had gone. "It was Mr. Montcrief," she told her father. "He wants you to go in to Penticton to his lawyer's office for a short meeting to wrap up some technicalities."

"Right now?" Mr. Simpson asked.

"Apparently."

"Would you like me to come with you?" Dad offered.

Mr. Simpson shook his head. "There's no need. Not if it's just technicalities."

Dad glanced at his watch. "Then, I think I'll take a run back to Vancouver and see if I can find any trace of Todd there." His voice was carefully casual. "It's not quite four. I can be there by early evening."

Brock Simpson's face broke into a relieved smile. "Would you, Syd? I'll give you a list of his friends and his haunts. When you find him, explain that it just makes things look worse if he stays away. Tell him we know he had nothing to do with that fire and that we'll stand back of him."

Dad nodded.

"Would you leave Lion and Bobbi here," Mr. Simpson suggested. "I think Chrissy would appreciate having company right now."

Again Dad nodded. "I'll be back as soon as I can," he promised.

Chapter 20

Todd stared at the tiny, ceiling-high window over his head. He tried to think back — to make sense of what had happened.

He could remember leaving the house last night, determined to check the equipment shed to see if he could find anything to link the fire with the person he'd followed out there the night before. All he'd been thinking about was getting there quickly and checking the ruins before the fire inspectors arrived in the morning and took away any evidence.

Talk about amateurs, he berated himself. Why hadn't he been more careful? Why hadn't he realized that anyone desperate enough to engineer a fire like that must be playing for big stakes? Instead, he set off so deep in thought he never even considered the possibility that he might be followed.

He hadn't even had a warning. Not a real one. He'd covered about half the distance to the burned-out equipment shed when he had a vague sensation of movement in the shadows beside him. But even as he was turning to see who it was, something thick and heavy and foul smelling had been thrown over his head. A moment later he'd felt his hands being lashed together behind his back. Then, something struck him hard on the back of the head, and he hadn't known anything more.

He continued staring at the tiny, ceiling-high window. He must have been knocked out for a long time, for the last thing he remembered it had been dark, and now he could see daylight filtering through the small opening, piercing the shadows in the shed where he was lying. But it didn't seem bright enough to be early morning sunlight or even noon time. It looked more like late afternoon.

Then had he been lying here ever since last night? Whatever had been put over his head was gone, but his hands were still tied and so were his feet, which explained why his whole body ached, he realized. It was from being tied so tightly. That was also why he was so cold. He had to do something before night came again, he told himself. But he felt too sick to worry about it right now.

Besides, his head ached too badly to be able to think clearly. He couldn't even make sense out of the weird shape of the ceiling over top of where he was lying. At first he'd thought it was some sort of loft, but as he continued to stare he realized there were neither steps nor a ladder leading up to it. Actually, he admitted to himself with a grin, if he didn't know better he'd think it was a huge tree stump dangling from the ceiling directly over where he was lying. Which proved his head was in no shape to think about anything. People didn't suspend tree stumps that probably weighed upwards of

400 pounds from the ceiling of deserted shacks. If his head was that scrambled, he'd better go back to sleep again till he could think properly.

He did.

Next time he awakened, it was again early morning. He could tell from the bright glitter in the tiny patch of sky he could see through that ceiling-high opening and from the terrible cold that seemed to have seeped into his very bones. He could no longer feel anything in his arms and legs — they were numb from the tightness of the cords that held him.

He continued to stare at the tiny opening, looking for anything familiar that would tell him where he had been taken. All he could see was about three inches of blue sky. But he must be still on the ranch, for he could hear some throaty grouse calling back and forth to each other not far away.

At least he could think more clearly now, he realized. Except for one silly thing. He still seemed to be seeing that crazy tree stump.

And now he could make out something else. The stump seemed to be sitting on a square of plywood, the inside edge of which was fastened to the wall with a hinge. The outside edge had a rope attached to it, holding it up level to the floor so the stump stayed balanced on top of the board. But the rope didn't just go over to the wall to be fastened there. Instead, it went straight up the wall and through a pulley attached to the ceiling. It continued across the ceiling and through another ceiling high pulley on the adjoining wall. Then, it went back down the inside wall and was firmly tied to the handle of the cabin door.

Todd didn't need anyone to spell out for him what that meant. As soon as someone pushed open the cabin door from outside, the pulley rope would go slack. The piece of plywood, held only by its hinge, would tip down and the heavy tree stump would roll off. It had a good eight metres to fall, Todd estimated, straight down — onto the tattered mattress where he had been tied and was unable to move.

All at once his headache and his sick stomach and even the possibility of freezing to death no longer seemed important. He felt a wave of panic. Obviously, whoever had burned down the equipment shed knew he'd been followed and probably suspected that he'd been recognized. And he'd rigged up the log and the pulley system to make sure that information wouldn't be passed on.

Chapter 21

At just about the same time that morning, Lion made his way in to breakfast to find his sister watching for him.

She hardly waited for him to sit down before saying earnestly, "We've got to take the horses and go —"

"Come on, Bobbi!" Lion reached for the cereal box. "They can exercise themselves for once out in that pasture. I've had enough riding to last for—"

"Not to exercise them! To go back out to that crop circle. Ever since I woke up, I've had this really weird feeling that it's important."

Lion gave his sister an even more disgusted look.

"I'm serious, Lion. I'm sure Todd didn't take off." Her voice tightened. "I'm sure he's still here somewhere, only I don't know where."

"What's that crop circle got to do with it?"

"I don't know." Bobbi gave him a self-conscious smile. "But I've got a funny feeling that something's wrong — that Todd is in danger — and that somehow the crop circle is important."

Lion's heart sank. They always ended up in trouble when his sister got one of those feelings that someone was in danger. Well, she could check it out alone. This time he wasn't having anything to do with it.

"Please, Lion," Bobbi continued, in the same self-conscious tone. "I want to ride out and see, only I'm scared to go alone."

Lion had been just preparing an iron clad excuse so he could avoid taking any part in this, but at Bobbi's words his resistance oozed away. Riding out to check that crop circle was the last thing he wanted to do, but how could a guy refuse when his sister said she needed him? Especially since Bobbi was always there for him when the situation was reversed. "Okay. Only this time," he quipped to hide his feelings, "I vote we take the road and not the short cut."

Bobbi grinned at him gratefully.

Half an hour later as they neared the north pasture, a gentle breeze started blowing. Moments later they reached the open meadow where the crop circle lay undisturbed.

Someone was there ahead of them. A girl in jeans and a floppy hat was standing by a fallen tree trunk just outside the outer rim of the circle and looking in their direction.

It was too much of a weird coincidence for Lion. He was ready to turn back, but Bobbi urged Brie on more quickly.

"I've been waiting, hoping you'd come," the girl said in a soft voice as they rode up.

Lion looked over sharply, more uncomfortable than he wanted to admit, for this was the first time he'd seen the girl close up, and it occurred to him that there was something about her that was different. Only what? She was dressed just like any other sixteen or seventeen year old and her hair was the same — long and wavy. Then …? Suddenly, Lion realized the answer. It was her eyes. They were light blue and penetratingly clear with depths that it seemed to him other people's eyes didn't have.

Quickly, he pushed that thought away, for it was crazy. Probably lots of people had eyes like that only he'd never noticed. Just the same, he found himself carefully avoiding her glance.

Bobbi had already jumped to the ground and was moving toward the girl. Determined to look unconcerned, Lion pulled Raj to a stand and also dismounted.

"Todd has disappeared!" Bobbi exclaimed in a quick, worried voice as soon as she was close enough. "Is that why you're here?"

Lion looked over at his sister in disgust. As if that girl would even know who Todd was, and he waited for the girl to say so.

Instead she nodded.

It was all the encouragement Bobbi needed. "Is he in danger?" she asked quickly, moving closer.

"Come on, Bobbi!" Lion protested. "She doesn't even know who Todd is, so how d'you expect her to know if he's in danger?"

"I don't know him," the girl agreed. "But I do know he is in danger and you must find him." She turned to Bobbi. "Because he is the only one who can save the valley."

129

"We've tried to find him, but we don't know where to look! Please, help us!"

The girl shook her head regretfully. "I'm just a visitor here, so I can't interfere. But you two know him, so you should be able to find him. Just think over everything that has happened."

"But —"

The girl's smile broadened. "Just think everything through carefully," she said again. "And as you do, remind yourself that nothing happens unless something else has happened first."

The words were so unexpected that Bobbi forgot all about feeling strange and frightened. "Our creative writing teacher told us that in school!" she exclaimed. "He told us Aristotle said it twenty-five hundred years ago!"

The girl's smile widened. "That's true. He did. And it's still good advice. If you think over everything that has happened starting with the things that happened first, you'll find the answer will be there." She started moving away.

"Why did you disappear that first time in the pasture?" Bobbi called after her.

The girl turned back. "Because I wanted to speak to you alone," she said softly.

"Was it you who helped us on that sand hill?"

Again the girl nodded. But now the smile had left her face. "I was hoping they would dig up all the things that had been buried there, that were poisoning the earth, but it seems they have forgotten."

"Is that why nothing will grow?"

The girl nodded. "But we mustn't waste time talking. You must find Todd before it is too late." Without giving Bobbi a chance to answer, she turned and moved across the meadow. A moment later she had disappeared among the trees.

At the same time the soft breeze faded away.

Chapter 22

"She must be that girl veterinarian Mr. Simpson was talking about!" Bobbi said in a wondering voice, gazing toward the trees where the girl had disappeared.

"Is that just a guess?" Lion quipped in what he hoped was a joking tone, for he didn't want his sister to know just how uneasy he was, "Or is it something else you just magically *know*?"

Bobbi didn't seem to hear. She was continuing to stare toward the trees where the girl had disappeared. "It isn't just the garbage hill that she's worried about," she said in the same far-away voice. "It's also those leg-hold traps and the poaching — and the worry that somebody might be trying to convert some of Mr. Simpson's best agricultural land into town lots. That's what she meant when she said the whole valley might be in danger."

Lion was getting more and more uncomfortable. He was frantically trying to think of a way to change the subject, when a new thought struck. "D'you think maybe she's some kind of animal rights activist? Or a Green Peace worker?"

Bobbi gave him a disgusted look.

"Okay, then you explain it," Lion retorted angrily.

For a moment longer, Bobbi hesitated, then said carefully, "As I told you, I think she's worried about those leg-hold traps and the poaching and about all the endangered animals in this area. I think she's afraid all the new people moving in will make changes to the valley that could affect the wildlife even more. I think she knows that though most people are aware of those things, they're not prepared to do anything about them." She paused, then, in a more self-conscious tone than ever, admitted, "I think that's why she wants us to find Todd, because she knows he really will try to do something about all those things before it's too late."

For a long moment there was silence, then, in an even softer voice, Bobbi added, "Maybe where she comes from it's already too late."

"Too late for what?"

"To save the animals. And maybe too late to save the air and the water, too."

If Lion had been uneasy before, now he felt prickles running up and down his spine. He was used to his sister having weird ideas, but this was too far out. "Next thing I suppose you'll try to convince me she's a Martian or an alien or some kind of space traveller," he blustered. "But that's crazy. How could she be from any different place when there wasn't the slightest thing science-fictionish about her. She looked and talked just like us?"

For a second it seemed Bobbi was going to argue, but she must have changed her mind. Instead, she said

133

quietly, "Please, Lion. It doesn't matter who we think that girl is or where she comes from. All that matters is finding Todd."

Lion felt his bluster ooze away. "You're right," he admitted with a sheepish smile. He dismounted as Bobbi had done. "So, what did she say again?"

Bobbi looked so grateful that, for a minute, he was afraid she might be going to come over and hug him. Would something like that ever make a guy feel dumb.

Bobbi must have guessed what he was thinking, for she gave him an amused grin, then, dropping Brie's lines so she could graze, sat down on the ground. "She said nothing happens unless something else has happened first."

"Was that Aristotle guy real, or somebody you two dreamed up?"

"Real. He was a philosopher who lived in Greece around 350 BC." Bobbi pulled at a bit of clover and put the stalk into her mouth.

Lion loosened Raj's girth, dropped his reins so the big horse could graze and sat down beside her. He was still uneasy about the girl, but the stuff she'd claimed Aristotle had said two thousand three hundred years ago made sense. Modern science proved it all the time. Nothing *did* happen except something else happened first. So maybe if they could just put the facts together properly ...

"All right, what d'we know?" he said, keeping his voice off-hand and casual, so his sister wouldn't think he was really buying into this psychic stuff.

134

Bobbi beamed at him gratefully. "You start."

"Okay. We know Todd has disappeared. We know the insurance people think it's because he set the fire with that toy horse, but Chrissy is positive he wouldn't have done that."

"So am I," Bobbi added quietly.

Actually, Lion was pretty sure Todd wouldn't have set the fire either. "But somebody set that fire and used that clock to do it —"

"Because they want to put the blame on Todd," Bobbi took over. "I should never have put the horse back," she added guiltily. "We knew somebody was down in the basement. I should have guessed it was to get the horse. Purely by luck I did keep him in my room that first night. If only I'd kept him there from then on."

"If you had, they'd have used something else," Lion said matter-of-factly. "Besides how could you have guessed that anybody would steal him? Forget about that and concentrate on what we know. Fact number one: somebody set the equipment shed on fire. Fact number two: whoever it was used Break Away as a detonator so no one would suspect who really had set it. Fact num —"

"I think you're saying it backward," Bobbi interrupted. "The person who set that fire used the horse clock as a detonator not to keep suspicion from falling on him, but to make sure it *did* fall on the Simpsons! Remember what Dad said about the insurance?" Bobbi's voice was starting to grow excited. "He said the insurance company wouldn't hold up payment of the insurance money even if they did suspect the fire had been deliberately set, so long as they knew it was someone else who had set it. It was only if they suspected that the Simpsons themselves had set it that they would hold up payment."

Lion was frowning. "Maybe that would have been important if the Simpsons were depending on the insurance money to replace the equipment, but they aren't. Mr. Montcrief is putting up the money. So what does it matter what the insurance people think?"

"But that didn't happen till just today. The person who set the fire wouldn't have known anything about Mr. Montcrief putting up the money."

"True."

"Let's start again," Bobbi said. "Fact number one: somebody deliberately set that fire and used Break Away as a detonator."

"Which meant coming into the basement to get him," Lion put in. "That's who it must have been in the basement that first night. Only, we came down into the basement before he had a chance to find him. So he waited."

Bobbi nodded. "Think how mad he must have been when we took Break Away instead and went back upstairs."

Lion laughed. "Though maybe he hadn't gone into the basement purposely to get the horse," he suggested. "Maybe he went down to look for something. And seeing us with Break Away put the idea in his head."

"That makes me feel even worse," Bobbi said softly. "If we hadn't asked to see Break Away —"

"Even if we hadn't, he still might have thought of him," Lion told her quickly. "But since he didn't get Break Away that first night, he probably figured he'd better come earlier the next evening before the house was locked up, because he wouldn't have dared use your window twice in a row. Only he came a bit too early and Todd heard him." Quickly he told his sister about seeing Todd at the top of the basement stairs then going down and following whoever it was outside.

"Why didn't you go too?"

Sheepishly, Lion admitted about his bare feet and pyjamas.

Bobbi gave him a teasing grin, but all she said was, "Could you see who it was Todd was following?"

"It was too dark."

"Was this just before the fire?"

"Not just before." Lion admitted. "This would have been at about ten o'clock. The fire didn't start till early the next morning." His face tightened into a frown. "Only it doesn't make sense if Todd followed somebody and realized what he was up to that he wouldn't have tried to stop him."

Bobbi nodded. "You'd think if he saw anybody going into the equipment shed, that he'd at least have tried to find out —" Suddenly she broke off and exclaimed instead, "But he wouldn't have!"

"He wouldn't have what?"

"He wouldn't have gone into the equipment shed!"

"Todd?"

"No, the person he was following."

"Yes, he would. How else could he have set that fire?"

"But not right then." Bobbi's voice was getting more and more excited. "Remember what Mr. Simpson told us about setting a clock timing device? If he was going to use Break Away to start the fire, he'd have had to get him ready first, and it would have been too risky to do that inside the equipment shed. Somebody might have come in for something and seen him. Because even if he'd already cut and prepared the wires, he'd still have had to glue them in place and wait for them to dry. Which would have taken time — maybe as much as an hour — even if he used fast drying Crazy Glue. He must have gone somewhere else to get the clock ready. And before he finally had everything arranged and went back to the equipment shed to set things up, Todd would have decided he'd lost him and gone home."

"*That* explains why Todd was so preoccupied and thoughtful all the next day," Lion exclaimed with a relieved smile. "He was probably trying to work out what was going on. It wouldn't have been till after the insurance man phoned Mr. Simpson to say they had some questions, that Todd would have realized the fire had been deliberately set."

"And he'd have guessed it must have been set by the person he'd been following!" Bobbi put in excitedly. "Then he didn't take off and run away! I was sure he hadn't. He must have realized his only chance to find out who had set the fire was to search the fire scene before the fire inspector came and took away anything suspicious. He must have realized he had to go right away or it would be too late, so he took off as soon as it was dark enough."

"Only this time maybe the roles were reversed." Lion took over, his voice low and tight. "Maybe this time the person who'd set the fire was tailing Todd. Maybe he waited for his chance, then locked Todd up somewhere and hid his truck so it would look as if he'd run away."

Again there was silence. This time it stretched out.

"I wish Dad hadn't gone to Vancouver," Bobbi said at last. "He can't possibly be back before late tomorrow — maybe not till the next day. Todd hasn't been seen since suppertime the night before last. That's more than thirty-six hours. What if —"

"Stop imagining the worst," Lion told her firmly. "Now that we've figured out what this is about, let's start again and see if we can work out where Todd could be hidden."

But after half an hour, both Bobbi and Lion were frightened all over again. It was all very well for that girl to tell them to consider all the facts and they'd have the answer, but what if by the time they came up with that answer it was too late?

Chapter 23

"I'm scared, Lion," Bobbi confessed in a frightened undertone as they got back on their horses and started home. "What if we can't find him?"

"We're sure to sooner or later," Lion told her with more cheerfulness than he felt. "But right now the best thing we can do is go back to the ranch and see if anyone else has heard anything. Maybe Dad has called by now."

Without another word being spoken, they both increased their pace. Half an hour later, they unsaddled their horses, rubbed them down, turned them loose, then headed for the ranch house.

But one look at Mr. Simpson's grey, haggard face as he came to the door to meet them, made it clear that no word had come from Todd.

"Has Dad called?" Bobbi asked quickly.

Mr. Simpson shook his head. "I haven't heard anything from him either."

But even as he spoke the sound of a car motor sounded in the drive. With a look of intense relief, Mr. Simpson started toward the door.

"Maybe that's Dad bringing Todd back," Lion whispered as he and Bobbi followed.

But it wasn't Dad's station wagon that was pulling to a stop at the end of the drive or Todd's red pick-up. It was the same mini sports car that had arrived a few days earlier. The same impeccably dressed figure, today in yellow and black, unwound herself from behind the wheel, but this time instead of concentrating on the ground and on keeping her clothes free from dirt and manure, her eyes were on Brock Simpson in the doorway.

"Oh, Brock, I'm so sorry," she said hurrying toward him, her face was soft with concern. "I've been in Vancouver the past few days and I just heard about the fire this morning. Is there anything I can do?"

At the mention of Vancouver, Brock Simpson's expression brightened. "Is Todd the one who told you about the fire? Were you talking to him? Is he still down there?"

Obviously puzzled, Lani shook her head. "I haven't seen him. I thought he was here visiting you and Chris."

The bleak, lost look returned to Mr. Simpson's face. "He was. But after the fire he disappeared. And the insurance adjusters —" He coughed to clear a funny note that had come into his voice, then continued, "The insurance adjusters are looking for him to ask a few questions. I'm afraid they think he has panicked and run away." As he was talking, he'd been piloting Lani back into the house and across the hall to the study. Now they moved inside and their voices no longer carried to where Bobbi and Lion were standing.

"He agrees with the insurance people," Bobbi said in a low worried voice. "He believes Todd panicked and ran away too. We've got to find him before —"

She broke off as brisk footsteps sounded on the walk outside. Suddenly, Mr. Montcrief arrived at the door, again in shining black riding boots and spotless jodhpurs, punctuating his strides with the flick of his riding crop against the side of one boot.

"Is Mr. Simpson around?" he asked, opening the door without bothering to knock and pushing past Bobbi. "In his study?" Again not waiting for an answer he moved toward it.

At the sound of Montcrief's voice, Brock Simpson reappeared in the doorway with Lani directly behind him.

A look of surprise came over Lani's face, changing almost immediately into a delighted smile."Warren! How nice!" she exclaimed, moving toward him.

Lion was watching Montcrief. He expected him to make up for ignoring Lani two days earlier with a smile or at least a "Hello," but instead he looked startled and almost angry as he moved past her toward Brock Simpson, who was still inside the study doorway.

Again Lani looked confused and hurt.

Brock Simpson noticed and his expression hardened. "Worried about those lessons for your girls, Montcrief? That why you've come?" His voice was unmistakably angry.

"As a matter of fact I've come about something else." Montcrief beat several more sharp taps with his crop against his boot, then said abruptly, "I've come to ask if

142

we can set up a shareholders' meeting in an hour's time — let's say at half-past one."

It was obvious that had been the last thing Brock Simpson had expected.

Lion was watching Lani. Rather than surprised, she looked uneasy — almost uncomfortable. Why? What was going on? Trying to be inconspicuous so the others wouldn't decide to move into the study and shut the door, Lion continued to watch.

"I suppose we can have a meeting if you want one," Brock Simpson was saying, trying to hide his obvious surprise. He turned to Lani and smiled down at her. "Would one-thirty suit you? After all, you should be there too as the second largest shareholder."

Lani smiled back at him gratefully and nodded. But it seemed to Lion that she was still uncomfortable and embarrassed. Several times she threw an apologetic glance at Montcrief, like a puppy who knew she'd done something wrong and was trying to get back in her owner's good graces.

But Montcrief had already started away.

Lani's face seemed to crumple as she watched him go, then she forced a smile. With an obvious effort at lightness she turned to Brock Simpson. "Last time I was here, Chrissy told me you had a new foal. You know how I love baby animals, Brock. Can I go down to the barn and have a look at him?"

Mr. Simpson seemed as relieved as she was at the change of mood and topic. "Of course. I'll walk down with you. Chrissy is there. She'll be delighted to show off her new baby." He turned to Lion and Bobbi who were still in the hallway. "Why don't you two come, too?"

Together they left the house and walked toward the barn.

It was obvious from Lani's delighted oohs and ahhhs that she really did mean what she'd said about loving baby animals. She had a string of questions to ask.

Bobbi motioned to Lion to move away. "Let's let them have a few minutes by themselves, okay?" she suggested in an undertone as she led the way back outside.

Ten minutes later Lani and Chrissy reappeared in the barn doorway. With a wave Lani moved toward her car.

"Don't forget to come back for the meeting!" Chrissy called. But as she watched her ex-stepmother drive away her smile changed to a frown.

"Is something wrong?" Bobbi asked as she and Lion moved over to join her.

"Not wrong," Chrissy hedged. "But weird. Lani told me about Mr. Montcrief asking Dad to call a shareholders' meeting." She continued to stare after the departing car. "Why would he do that? It doesn't make sense."

Lion grinned. "It does if you remember what you told us about Montcrief's 'I-am-a-big-important-land-owner' fixation. He probably asked for the meeting because he thinks it will raise his image with his friends. Now he can tell everybody he's tied up all day because of the meeting, and it will sound as if he's a major share holder."

Chrissy didn't even smile. "It's not only the meeting itself that's weird," she continued in the same worried tone. "It's how Lani acted. For some reason she seemed to be worried about it."

"Did she say so?" Bobbi asked quickly.

"Not in words. But she acted that way. I'd be telling her about Break Away, and suddenly it would seem that she was no longer listening — she'd be staring back over at the house as if she was thinking about something else. Finally, I asked her if something was wrong. I thought she'd say of course not and change the subject, but she didn't. Instead, she gave me this funny look and said that she hoped she wasn't being too hasty. That maybe she should have waited longer."

"Waited longer for what?"

"I asked her that, but she didn't answer. All she would say was that everything would probably turn out just fine, and for me to forget what she'd said." Chrissy smiled. "Maybe I'm just imagining things." As if determined to put the whole thing out of her mind she turned her attention back to the new foal and its mother."

But Chrissy's comments had started Lion thinking. Waiting just long enough to make sure that Chrissy really was once again concentrating on the foal, he moved closer to Bobbi. "Come outside for a bit, okay?" he said in an undertone.

If Bobbi had been planning to object, one look at her brother's face made her change her mind. She followed him out into the ranch yard. "What's wrong?" she asked quietly as soon as they were far enough away to avoid being overheard.

"Let's go down to the pasture and pretend we're checking on Brie and Raj, okay? I don't want Chrissy to hear, because it'll only worry her."

"Then we'd better give them a brushing while we talk, so it will look authentic," Bobbi said, stopping to get curry combs and brushes from the tack box inside the horse trailer. "Okay, now we look the part. So tell me what's wrong."

For a minute, as they started walking again, Lion was silent, wondering how best to explain what he was thinking. He said at last, "Didn't it strike you as strange that Mr. Montcrief was so unfriendly to Lani a few minutes ago when he came into the house?"

"What do you mean?"

"Lani seemed really pleased to see him, but he looked almost angry — as if he was annoyed that she was there. If she was married to Mr. Simpson for three years and Montcrief was their neighbour, the two of them must be friends."

"Not necessarily," Bobbi retorted with a grin. They'd reached the pasture. She opened the gate so they could move inside. "I know lots of people who aren't friends with their neighbours."

Lion ignored the joke. "Why would Lani seem so pleased to see him if he wasn't the least bit pleased to see her?"

"Who knows? But what does it matter?" She turned

her attention to the two horses who had seen them approaching and were now walking to meet them.

"It could matter a lot, if Mr. Montcrief was angry because he hadn't wanted Lani to know about the shareholder's meeting," Lion said carefully.

Bobbi had been patting Brie, but at that she turned back abruptly. "You mean that maybe he didn't want her to be there?"

Lion nodded.

"Why?"

"I don't know," Lion admitted sheepishly.

Bobbi's eyes lifted briefly skyward in resignation. "Then stop worrying about it." Turning back to Brie, she started to brush her gleaming chestnut coat.

Absentmindedly, Lion started brushing Raj, but it was clear his thoughts weren't on the horse. "There's something else," he continued. "Remember that day Dad and Mr. Simpson came back from the bank to tell us about Montcrief putting up the money to replace the equipment at only half the interest that the bank would have charged? Didn't that strike you as out of character?"

"Out of character how?"

"Remember what Chrissy said about Montcrief being a real wheeler-dealer business promoter? Doesn't it strike you as strange that he'd lend that much money out at half of what he could have charged?"

"Not if he's a good friend, and not if he has dreams of being an important country gentleman and having a voice in running a big operation like this ranch."

"Maybe," Lion agreed. "But I keep remembering what that girl said about nothing happening except something else happening first."

Again Bobbi stopped brushing.

"I wonder," Lion went on in the same careful voice, "what might have happened just before Montcrief decided to put the money up for that loan."

"That's easy. The fire happened," Bobbi retorted acidly.

"No, after that."

"Maybe Mr. Simpson asked the bank for a loan and they said no."

Lion shook his head. "He told Chrissy he hadn't had to ask the bank for a loan because Mr. Montcrief came forward and offered."

"Okay, so if that didn't happen first, you tell me what did?"

Lion's grin grew even more self-conscious. "That's the trouble. I don't know."

Bobbi gave him another disgusted glance and went back to her brushing. A few minutes later, she glanced at her watch. "Do you think Mr. Simpson might let us sit in on that meeting?"

"He might — especially if Dad's still not back."

"Let's go and see. It's a quarter past one. We can just get there in time." Giving Brie one final brush, she turned and started back toward the pasture gate.

Lion followed.

Chapter 24

At exactly twenty-five minutes past one, Mr. Montcrief and Kurt reappeared in the Willow Creek ranch yard. There was no sign of Lani.

At one thirty Brock Simpson led them into the study, beckoning to Chrissy, Bobbi and Lion to come in too.

For a moment a flush of annoyance came into Mr. Montcrief's face. It seemed to Lion that he was about to protest, but he must have thought better of it, for without a word he followed the others into the study and sat down.

The meeting was called to order. It was low key and friendly. Mr. Simpson said he was sorry Lani hadn't come, but that she never had been interested in business matters. Then he read the balance sheet and the financial statement, made reference to the loan to replace the equipment, expressed his gratitude to Montcrief for putting up the funds, then announced his general plans for the coming year. "Now, I wish to welcome our new temporary shareholder," he said, smiling at Mr. Montcrief. "Have you any questions? Or is there anything you would like to bring before this meeting before we adjourn?"

Montcrief's polite inconspicuous manner disappeared. His shoulders straightened. He settled back more comfortably in his chair. "Not exactly a temporary shareholder," he corrected in an amused tone. "I think you'll have to get used to seeing me at these meetings, Simpson. In fact, I think you'll have to get used to seeing me chair them, for the situation isn't quite what you think."

Brock Simpson's expression had tightened. An angry line had appeared around the corners of his mouth.

"I don't know if Lani has mentioned it to you," Montcrief went on in the same smug tone, "but we are planning to get married. The wedding is set for the day after tomorrow. Earlier today I had my lawyer draw up a pre-nuptial agreement giving us both equal ownership of all our individual assets — including Lani's shares in the ranch."

In the stunned silence that followed, Lion glanced quickly at Bobbi. He knew she was thinking exactly what he was. That *that* was what had happened just before Montcrief offered to put up the money for the loan — Lani had agreed to marry him!

The colour had drained from Mr. Simpson's cheeks.

"You'll remember at the meeting today," Montcrief continued, no longer even trying to hide his smug self-satisfaction, "that I was the one who casually suggested three percent of the ranch shares as collateral for the loan. It was obliging of you and the bank to agree so willingly." His smirking smile broadened. "As a result, Lani and I together now control fifty-one percent of the

150

shares, leaving you forty-nine percent. Sorry, if it is a shock to you, but that's business, you know." He paused, then added, "Since I am now chief shareholder, and intend to take over as chairman and decision maker, I've arranged for my lawyer to come over a little after half-past four this afternoon to settle the details." He paused, then with an even wider grin continued, "You'll be pleased to know that I have exciting plans for the ranch." He looked around as if to enjoy the effect of his words. "I've been making some inquiries at the Land Office — in your name of course."

Again Lion glanced at Bobbi. Had Montcrief also been the person making inquiries at the bank, pretending to be Mr. Simpson? Had he done it on purpose to arouse the bank's suspicions, so they wouldn't jump at granting Mr. Simpson a loan when the trap was laid and he had to find extra money? Then Montcrief must have been the person in those ID shots. He also must have been the person in Bobbi's room, coming to steal those pictures since he knew where they were. He'd walked into the house uninvited that first afternoon just as Mr. Simpson was telling Dad where he had put them.

"Of course I intend to make some *improvements*," Montcrief was continuing in the same gloating tone. "First, I'll add some fencing to keep those useless wild animals away." A wry smile pulled at his lips. "It means putting an end to a profitable little business I've been running selling poaching rights to a friend, but that was starting to get a little dangerous anyway."

That's who had been poaching, Lion realized. Not Todd or Kurt, but someone who was paying Montcrief a rake-off!

"Then I plan to drain that big pond and divert the creek," Montcrief continued, his voice ringing with self-satisfaction, "so a major road can be built. You see, I intend to turn that big meadow into a high-priced housing development."

The shocked looks on the faces gazing back at him seemed to give Montcrief even greater amusement. "In case you're wondering how I expect to get approval for all this, I should explain that I've a friend in the Land Reserve Commission. I think for a small share of the eventual profits, he will be glad to help me push it through."

For a moment Mr. Simpson was too badly shaken to speak. He glanced hopelessly over at Chrissy. Then, pulling himself together with an effort, he said stiffly, "Since, for the moment at least I am still chairman, I declare this meeting adjourned." His voice didn't sound like his. "It will reconvene at half past four when your lawyer arrives." Without another word he left the room, one arm around Chrissy's shoulders.

Bobbi and Lion followed.

Chapter 25

"If only your dad were here to advise me," Mr. Simpson muttered to Bobbi in a stunned tone as they crossed the hall. "As it stands I don't know if there is anything I can do. If Montcrief and Lani really are getting married, and if she's signed a pre-nuptial agreement —"

"If only Todd would come back," Chrissy put in, sounding close to tears.

Bobbi glanced at her watch. "It's just two. That meeting isn't till half past four. Lion and I will go out again," she said with more confidence than she was feeling, "and maybe this time we can find him."

"If only you could," Mr. Simpson told her with a small smile. "Though, it won't make any difference to Montcrief's scheme."

"But it could!" Chrissy countered. For the first time, a hint of life had come back into her face. "If Lion and Bobbi can find Todd, and if he can prove that he didn't set the fire, then the insurance company will pay the premium and you can cancel that loan!"

For a second Mr. Simpson looked almost hopeful, then the lost look returned. "Unfortunately, the evidence is against him." he told her softly.

"But he might have found something that would change that!" Chrissy persisted.

"If he has, that would explain why he's disappeared!" Lion put in with sudden excitement. Quickly, he told Mr. Simpson and Chrissy about seeing Todd leaving the house the evening before the fire, following someone who'd been in the basement. "Next day he must have started wondering if the person he'd been following could have had something to do with the fire. So maybe that night he decided to go back out to see if he could spot anything in the ruins before the fire inspectors arrived and took over." He paused, then finished carefully, "Even if he didn't find anything, maybe the person who set the fire thinks Todd knows the truth, and so is deliberately keeping him from coming back and telling anybody."

At Lion's words new life came back into Mr. Simpson's face as well as Chrissy's.

"Come on, Lion, let's go," Bobbi said quickly before Mr. Simpson could say it would be too dangerous. Beckoning to Lion to follow, she led the way outside.

At the same moment, Kurt appeared from around the side of the house.

Had he been standing by the open study window listening, Lion wondered in alarm.

But Kurt wasn't paying any attention to them at all. His attention was on Chrissy standing in the doorway, and he was smirking. "When you're talking to that brother of yours, tell him he was smart to run away and

154

he'll be even smarter to stay away, because now that my dad is taking over the ranch, things are gonna be different. Your brother's cushy little poaching hobby can be forgotten."

Lion moved forward. "You should have been listening at that meeting, Kurt," he said at his dryest. "Didn't you hear? It's your dad who's been running that cushy little poaching hobby —"

Bobbi caught his arm. "Argue with him later," she said in an urgent undertone. "We haven't time now."

Reluctantly, Lion fell into step beside her.

As they walked to the pasture, neither of them spoke, and the silence continued as they saddled the horses. But as they set out again on the familiar trails that circled the ranch, Bobbi said thoughtfully, "You were right about it having been out of character for Montcrief to put up that money for the loan at such a low interest rate. Well, something else was out of character, too."

Lion looked over sharply. "Like what?"

"It was out of character for somebody to have scared us away from that old cabin three days ago."

Lion gave her a disgusted look. "No it wasn't. Whoever was there obviously didn't want us seeing those leg-hold traps."

"But you said yourself they looked so old and rusty that they might not even work any more."

It was true, Lion realized. "So, what are you saying?"

"That there had to be an important reason why the person watching us gave himself away, because it could

155

have meant trouble. He obviously wasn't supposed to be on Mr. Simpson's property, or he wouldn't have hidden in the first place."

That thought hadn't occurred to Lion. "You're saying he deliberately gave himself away to distract us because there was something else in the cabin beside the old traps that he might not have wanted us to see?"

"Maybe. We didn't see anything, but we were so upset at seeing those traps we probably didn't really look. But I can't help wondering if it wasn't connected to any particular thing inside the cabin at all, just to the cabin itself."

For a long moment there was silence. Then, Lion said carefully, "Maybe we still haven't gone back far enough." His thoughts were racing. "What if the thing that happened first was just that Todd came home? Chrissy said they weren't expecting him till the end of the summer. When he turned up, she was really surprised, and Kurt was too."

Bobbi's face lit with excitement. "Maybe that was it! Maybe that was what Kurt and his dad had been waiting for, because everything depended on it! Everything else was set. They'd made their plans. First, that string of accidents so the ranch would be in financial straits. Next, Montcrief getting Lani to agree to marry him so he'd have control of her shares —"

"Then planting that barbed wire," Lion took over, "right in the middle of that thick patch of bracken and wild roses. Chrissy said it was so well hidden that no horse would have noticed it till too late. They knew sooner or later Epic was sure to wander into it, and when he did, that'd be the end of any plans the Simpsons might have had to sell him as a last resort if they needed money to tide them over."

"Then finally the fire," Bobbi added. "If the Simpsons were suspected of setting it, the insurance company was sure to hold up payment, and Mr. Simpson would have no choice but to accept Montcrief's offer of a loan."

"But it all hinged on Todd coming home." Lion's voice had grown tight, and he spaced each word carefully. "Because right from the start, they must have been planning to set Todd up to take the blame. That's probably why they used Break Away to make the timer device. They knew it would immediately throw suspicion on Todd because he was the timer specialist."

"And to make sure he didn't somehow come up with a convincing alibi," Bobbi added, "they arranged for him to disappear right after the fire so it would look as if he'd run away."

For a long moment after that they rode in silence. Then in a low, shaking voice Bobbi said, "I'm scared, Lion. If we don't find him soon it could be too late."

Chapter 26

They'd been so busy thinking and talking that they'd been letting the horses pick their own way and set their own pace. But at Bobbi's words, Lion tightened his reins and pulled Raj to a halt. "You're right. We've got to find him right now, or it could be too late. Let's try one more 'what-happened-first,' okay?"

Bobbi nodded.

"We agreed Kurt and his dad had set up this really complicated plan with everything set to happen in order and were just waiting for Todd to come home to set the trap, right?"

Bobbi nodded.

"But before you can set a trap for somebody, you've got to know what you're going to do with them afterward, right?"

"Mmmm-hmmm."

"Well, maybe that out-of-character business of somebody giving themselves away just to chase us from a ramshackle deserted cabin is the key we've been looking for." Lion's voice grew more excited. "Maybe whoever was there chased us away because they were planning to use that cabin to put Todd in, and maybe they were already starting to get things ready."

"Only we were so upset at seeing those traps," Bobbi took over, "that we didn't look at anything else!"

Without another word being spoken they turned onto the trail leading to the big pond and put the horses into a ground-eating canter.

Several minutes later they could see the pond ahead of them and just beyond, protected by its windbreak of poplar trees, the dilapidated shack.

Only it wasn't dilapidated looking any longer.

"Look!" Lion exclaimed, staring.

The door was no longer hanging drunkenly by its bottom hinge, and the boards that had been half on and half off the windows were now firmly nailed in place.

Slowly, they approached the cabin. When they were just twenty or thirty paces away, Lion slowed Raj to a halt, swung down, dropped his reins, then with a firm order to stand, he started toward the cabin.

"Wait!" Bobbi called sharply.

Lion didn't even hear.

He'd reached the door. Quickly, he pushed at the latch, but something must have been caught for it didn't want to open. He pushed harder, then began using his shoulder against the door itself. "I think he's in there!" he called excitedly back to Bobbi. "I'm sure he's in there! I can hear someone!"

By this time Bobbi had dismounted and had run up beside him. But instead of trying to help with the door, she caught his arm and pulled him backward.

"Cut it out Bobbi! Leave me alone! Can't you hear him calling for help! Let me see what's holding —"

"He's not calling help, he's calling don't!" Bobbi cried, continuing to pull at Lion's arm. "Stop, Lion! Wait till we make sure!"

With a shocked look Lion stopped pushing against her. Was she right? Could Todd have been calling *Don't*? Together they stood motionless and listened.

"Don't push … booby-trapped …" a faint, hoarse voice came back to them.

Lion stared at his sister in horror. If it hadn't been for her …

"Before we do anything else, we've got to find out what he means," Bobbi told him. For the past few seconds, she'd been studying the cabin walls. "Look, there's a small ventilation opening," she said, pointing high up under the roof, directly over the repaired cabin door.

"That's way too high up to see through," Lion objected.

"You're right. Maybe there's something else." As she spoke, Bobbi began circling the cabin. A moment later she called excitedly from around the back, "Lion! Come here! There's a space between the boards! Can you climb up?"

Lion hurried around the cabin to join her.

The space she was pointing at was a good metre above his head, and there was nothing around to stand on.

Then, he remembered Raj. Bringing the big horse around from the front where he'd been waiting, Lion positioned him directly below the crack in the boards, dropped his reins onto the ground, then again in his most imperious tone, gave him the order to *stand*.

Raj looked around at him.

"So, stand! Okay?" Lion said again.

Raj didn't move.

Lion put one foot into the stirrup and stepped up. But instead of swinging the other leg over and sitting in the saddle, he stepped up onto it with both feet, struggling to regain his balance on the curved surface.

Again Raj swung his head around and looked at him.

"You move and you're dog food," Lion threatened. To be on the safe side, he gathered himself, ready to jump in case Raj should decided this was his chance to play a new round of one-upmanship.

Raj continued to look amused, but he didn't move.

Slowly Lion straightened.

The crack was still several inches above eye level. Trying to ignore the thought of what would happen if Raj decided to take off, he stepped up onto his tiptoes. At last his eyes were level with the crack.

Once glance was enough to shake him badly. He saw Todd tied onto a threadbare mattress directly under a sheet of plywood that was held perpendicular to the wall by a rope and balancing a heavy tree stump on top of itself.

For a moment he couldn't take his eyes off the small square of plywood, which was all that seemed to be keeping the huge tree stump from falling. Then he let his glance follow the rope. It threaded its way up the wall, through a pulley, across the ceiling, down the other wall, through another pulley, then was fastened to the door handle. He knew enough about pulleys from school to know what would happen if the door opened and the rope went slack.

The knot the rope made around the door latch was probably all that had stopped the door from opening when he first pushed it, he realized. What if that knot hadn't been in the way? What if the door had opened easily? What if he'd pushed harder?

"What can you see, Lion? What is it?" Bobbi called impatiently.

He didn't answer. In fact he hardly heard. For all at once, he was no longer worried by the thought of what would happen if the door opened. What was terrifying him was the look of the rope itself. Where it passed through one of the pulleys two of its three strands were frayed right through. Only one strand was continuing to hold up the weight of that huge tree stump.

"What is it, Lion?" Bobbi called again, her voice worried.

Carefully letting himself back down onto his heels, Lion crouched back down onto the saddle, then jumped to the ground. In a tight, frightened voice he told Bobbi what he'd seen.

"You think the rope is fraying with the weight?" Bobbi asked in a scared voice.

Lion nodded. "They'd never have taken a chance on using it if had been frayed at the start in case it had broken while they'd been setting things up."

"Then there isn't time to go for help." Bobbi's voice was tight. "If the rope has frayed that much in just a couple of days, it could fray the rest of the way at any moment. We can't take a chance."

"But there's no way we can rescue Todd ourselves —"

"Yes, there is," Bobbi glanced over at Raj's saddle. "For once that lasso rope you always insist on carrying is going to be useful. You've got to climb up and snare the pulley rope, then tie it with your lasso so it can't slip while I open the door and get Todd out."

"That rope is holding up a four- or five-hundred-pound stump!" Lion objected. "If it's heavy enough to be fraying that rope, how d'you expect me to be able to hold it while you open the door?"

"I don't. But I'm hoping Raj can."

"Pardon?"

"It's our only chance. There isn't time to ride back to the ranch for help because that rope could fray through the rest of the way at any moment. Besides, if Mr. Montcrief or Kurt saw us, they might try to stop us. Please, Lion! We've got to try!"

Bobbi was right. It was their only chance. But what if they couldn't hold the rope? Or what if that last strand was fraying through right this moment —

He pushed that thought away. Instead, with what he hoped would pass for humour, he managed, "I told you cowboys always carry lassos. So what do I do?"

"Climb up, snare the pulley rope and tie it with your lasso."

163

"Through that little crack in the boards? Don't be dumb. Besides that crack is on the back wall, nowhere near the pulley rope."

"No, not the crack in the hoards. You've got to use that ventilation hole under the roof." Bobbi pointed. "It's directly over top of the door and the pulley rope runs right under it."

"But that's miles over my head. Even if I stood on Raj, I'd never be able to reach it!"

"You could if you climbed up in those trees then jumped down onto the roof." Bobbi pointed to the clump of poplars that had obviously been planted by an early occupant as a windbreak to shelter the cabin. "You could lie flat on the roof just above that ventilation opening and reach down inside to snare the pulley."

"I'm scared of heights!"

"Please, Lion. There isn't time to argue. That rope could fray through at any moment." Bobbi paused, then with a crooked smile added, "And I'm scared of heights too."

Lion gave her what he hoped was a withering look. He already knew she wasn't any better on heights than he was. As for climbing trees, she hadn't done nearly as much of that as he had. A guy couldn't let his sister do something he was too scared to do himself.

Getting his lasso off the saddle, he picked the biggest of the cottonwood trees growing close against the cabin and climbed up.

That was the easy part. The hard part was letting go

of the branch he was perched on and dropping down onto the roof. What if he slipped and rolled off? What if the ceiling boards of the cabin were rotten and broke when he hit them and he fell right through?

Well, if that was going to happen he'd just as soon not see, he decided. Closing his eyes tight he took a deep breath and jumped.

He felt the jar of the rough worn roof shingles beneath his feet. He'd made it! He hadn't fallen off and the cabin roof hadn't broken. The worst was over. Now it was just a question of crawling across the roof to the far side …

The worse wasn't over. The worst was just beginning. He'd never realized before how awful it felt when you were scared of heights to have to peer over the edge of a roof with your head pointing down while you reached a full arm's length into a ventilation hole to try to snare a dangling pulley rope! For a couple of minutes he was sure he was going to fall. If only he had somebody to sit on his legs. He remembered reading somewhere that a guy's shoulders, chest, head and arms were the heaviest part of his body. Didn't that mean that in this position mere body weight alone would make him topple off?

Quickly he pushed that idea away. It hadn't happened yet, he told himself sternly, so maybe if he was quick —

"Hurry, Lion!" Bobbi called up from below.

At last his shaking fingers felt the thick, sisal rope. Frantically, he grabbed hold. Then, careful not to shift too much body weight in case that was all it needed to topple him over, he took his lasso rope and wrapped

165

one end of it three times, as tightly as he could, around the pulley rope so it wouldn't slip. He was hoping that even if it did slip, it would slip slowly — by which time he and Bobbi should have Todd pulled out of the way.

Now, to get back down.

He started inching upwards and backward, slowly letting out the lasso, one end of which was now firmly tied to the pulley rope inside the cabin. At last his whole body was once again on the roof. Then, using the same overhanging tree as a ladder, he climbed back down, continuing to let the lasso rope out as he went so that, though it was tied to the pulley rope, it wasn't yet pulling against it.

At last to his relief he felt his feet touch ground.

His sister must have been just as scared as he was, for as soon as he was safely down she ran forward and hugged him in a frantic squeeze. "I was scared you'd fall," she mumbled, still squeezing. "I was afraid that maybe —"

"Hey! Don't be dumb! I'm fine! So cut it out. Okay?" He pulled free.

Actually, he'd have liked to hug his sister back and tell her that he'd been terrified too, that he'd been sure he was gonna fall head first over the edge of the roof, but a guy couldn't admit something like that. Anyway, from the warm smile that came into Bobbi's eyes, he had a feeling she knew exactly how he'd been feeling without needing to be told. "So, now what d'we do?" he asked in what he hoped was a normal tone.

"Fix up a pulley system of our own." As she spoke Bobbi took the free end of the lasso rope that Lion was still holding and moved toward Raj. "I just hope he hasn't forgotten his training. Remember when Dad first gave him to you, he told us that he was a pretty hotshot cutting horse?"

"So he can cut steers from a herd," Lion agreed. "He proved that up in Wells. But how's that gonna help us now?"

"Cutting cattle isn't the only thing good cow ponies can do," She gave Raj a pat, then began tying the end of the lasso rope firmly around the horn on Lion's stock saddle. There was still a little slack in the rope but not much.

"What else can cow ponies do?"

"You've been to the rodeo. You've seen the cowboys in the steer wrestling competitions and in the calf roping events. Well, those events just imitate what cowboys and their horses do all the time out on a ranch whenever they have to brand a cow or give it a vaccination or whatever. The cowboy ropes the calf or the steer, snugs the end of the lasso rope tight around the saddle horn, then gives his horse the order to pull back and hold the rope taut so the calf can't run away. Then all the cowboy has to do is hand-over-hand his way down the rope till he reaches the cow, then do whatever needs doing."

"If you think this horse can do that, you're a dreamer," Lion retorted sarcastically.

"Let's hope you're wrong," Bobbi told him, the worry rushing back into her voice. She checked to make

167

sure the lasso was firmly tied around the saddle horn, then stepped "So, mount him, okay? Back him till the rope is taut. Then make him keep pulling back so the rope stays taut. And while you do that, I'll slowly edge open the cabin door. The important thing is to keep the pulley rope from moving even an inch till I can run in and pull Todd out from under that stump."

Lion made no move to mount.

"Hurry, Lion! There might not be much more time!"

Lion continued to stand motionless. "I'm okay on the getting mounted part, and pretty good on the backing him till the rope is taut," he said, "But I'm not too clear on the rest."

"Come on, Lion! Stop playing games! We've got to hurry."

"I'm not playing games. I mean it. What order do I use?"

"I just told you. First —"

"I mean what order do I give Raj? What do I say so he knows that when the weight suddenly comes on the rope as you open the door, that I don't want him moving forward as he's trained to do when he feels a rope pulling him? How do I make him understand that I want him to back up and pull the other way to keep the rope taut?"

With a shock Bobbi realized what Lion was saying. Horses were trained to follow the pull on a rope, not to hold back and fight against it. Raj's instinct would be to do exactly the opposite of what they wanted. "But cattle horses hold ropes taut for calf roping all the time!" she protested. "There has to be an order that they understand!"

"Great. But what is it? What d'you figure I should say to warn Raj what's going to happen?" Lion's voice tightened. "Because all it's gonna take for that stump to come crashing down is one split second while the rope holding up the plywood board goes slack."

Bobbi's face blanched. "I don't know what the command is. Maybe Raj doesn't need one. Maybe he will just do it automatically."

"What if he doesn't? We can't take a chance. If you open that door and Raj doesn't pull back, we could get Todd killed."

For a long moment there was silence, then Bobbi said, "Do some tests and see if you can find the right words to make Raj understand. Give him some commands."

"Commands like what?"

"Pull! maybe, or hold!" Bobbi suggested.

Lion tried each of them with no result. Raj continued to stand where he was, making no move to move backward and tighten the rope.

Bobbi glanced at her watch. "It's half past three. We're running out of time. That meeting is scheduled for half past four. If we don't get Todd back and prove that he's innocent, Mr. Simpson could lose control of the ranch." She looked frantically at Lion. "Try the commands again!"

"Pull!" Lion shouted the command this time.

Nothing happened.

"Hold!"

Still Raj didn't move. In fact he was starting to look bored.

"You stupid, good-for-nothing horse!" Lion bellowed, "Get Back!" At the same moment he yanked backward on the reins.

Raj jumped back, snapping the rope tight and pulling against it to keep it that way.

"It worked!" Bobbi cried excitedly. "That's the command! He knows what we want! He remembers! Say it again and keep pulling him back while I open the door!"

"Back! Get back!" Lion ordered again, timing it so the order came just as Bobbi reached the cabin door and pushed against it, and at the same second giving a fresh tug on the reins.

Suddenly, the door sprang open.

"Get back!" Lion shouted again as the rope attached to his saddle horn jerked fiercely.

For an awful second, he was afraid the weight might be more than Raj could hold or that as Raj jumped backward the sudden snap might be all that was needed to fray through that last strand of rope. But it held. As Raj jumped backward the plywood board that had been starting to fall came back up again—and leveled. The heavy stump settled again on its supporting platform. In the next moment, Lion could see Bobbi backing out the doorway, holding the still-tied Todd under his arms and dragging him out the door behind her.

"Is he okay?" Lion called anxiously.

"I'm … not … sure," Bobbi replied, out of breath. "But I … think … so."

"Can Raj let the rope go now?"

"No! Not yet!" Bobbi had Todd well clear of the doorway. Settling him back down on the ground, she turned to Lion. "Can Raj keep holding the stump weight for a minute longer? Just till I shut the door? Then no one will know we've found him. They'll think he's still inside." As she spoke she moved back and securely closed the cabin door. "Okay, now you can tell Raj to relax," she said.

"How?" Lion wanted to know for Raj was continuing to strain to keep the rope taut.

Bobbi was so relieved that the danger was over that she started to giggle. "I don't know that command either, but if you tell him good boy and use your heels to move him forward, he's bound to understand that he can stop pulling back."

"Unless he's so dumb he's waiting for a calf to materialize at the other end of the rope," Lion said, but the words were contradicted by the quick grateful pat he gave Raj's sweating neck and the warmth of the *Good boy*, that accompanied it.

Raj moved forward as commanded, then as the rope went slack and the pressure came off his saddle horn, he shook himself furiously, cast a quick look back at Lion as if to say: Enough of this cowboy stuff. Then he dropped his head looking for something to eat as a reward for all his hard work.

By this time Bobbi had managed to untie the ropes that were binding Todd's arms and legs. "Are you okay?" she asked anxiously.

Todd's face was ashen, and it was clear he was only barely conscious, but he forced a smile and nodded.

Bobbi turned back to Lion. "The first thing is to hide your lasso rope."

"How can I hide it? It's still tied to the pulley inside the cabin." He wasn't about to admit it to his sister, but there was no way he was climbing back up onto the roof and hanging over to untie the rope. It had been bad enough last time, and that had just been a case of snaring the pulley rope. This time would be way worse, for the knot he'd tied around the pulley rope would have been yanked tight by the pulling. It would take both hands and all his strength to undo it.

"You don't have to untie it. Leave the end that's tied to the pulley, but undo the end on your saddle horn and tuck the rope down in the grass. With luck nobody will notice it."

"But why do you want it to look as if Todd is still in there?"

"Because they may have more tricks. We may need to be able to prove that they were prepared to kill Todd in order to keep him from talking, and that booby-trapped door is the proof. Also," she added, a twinkle coming into her eyes, "if one of them decides to come out to check that he's still inside, they're not likely to look too closely."

172

Lion grinned. His sister was right. He had an idea it would take more than just curiosity for Kurt or his dad to want to open that door.

Bobbi was once again leaning over Todd. Several times he'd tried to say something, but no words had come out. Now he raised a hand and pointed toward the bottle of drinking water she always carried clipped to her belt. "Of course!" she exclaimed. "Two days out here without anything to eat or drink! No wonder you're too dry to talk!" And handing him the bottle, she helped him sit up to drink.

In long, thirsty gulps, Todd drained it. He smiled sheepishly as he handed the empty bottle back. "Sorry. Guess I should have left some for somebody else." His voice was still slow and hoarse, but the words were clear.

Bobbi continued to smile down at him warmly.

"Oh, no," Lion muttered disgustedly. "Here we go again."

Bobbi paid no attention. "I'm just sorry we were so dumb. We never thought to bring along something for you to eat." Then the realization that Todd was safe brought such a wave of relief that she started to giggle. "We're like the people in that joke — who went to church to pray for rain and not one of them brought along an umbrella. We knew you'd been lost for two days, yet we came out looking and never even thought about bringing something for you to eat and drink if we found you."

It was Todd's turn to grin.

"Come on, you guys," Lion told them crossly. "Do your visiting later, okay? We've got to get back."

His words recalled Bobbi. Quickly, she looked at her watch. "We're too late! It's almost four! We'll never get back in time. The meeting is set for four-thirty!"

"What meeting?" Todd managed, his voice stronger but still hoarse.

Quickly, Bobbi explained.

Todd's face tightened as he listened.

"Someone has got to get back there," Lion put in, "or Mr. Simpson will lose control of the ranch." He turned to Bobbi. "The only way to make it by four-thirty is to gallop, which means you've got to go ahead. Todd and I'll follow on Raj as quickly as we can. But you've got to find some way to stall the meeting. Start talking and refuse to sit down like they do in those movies when somebody organizes a filibuster. Keep talking till we get there."

Bobbi nodded. With one last worried smile at Todd, she mounted Brie and started off.

"Only don't let them suspect Todd's no longer in that cabin!" Lion called after her. "Don't let them know we've found him. The last thing we need is for somebody to come out and decide to put both of us back under that stump. Make some excuse about why I'm not there … say I'm not coming … so they don't wonder about me."

Again Bobbi nodded.

Todd and Lion watched her go, then with difficulty, Lion helped Todd up onto Raj and swung up behind him.

At the extra weight, Raj braced his hind legs, then threw Lion a pained glance backward.

"Stop complaining," Lion told him in an unsympathetic tone, then he relented and gave the big horse a pat. "We'll go slowly," he compromised. "And I'll give you some extra oats when we get back."

Raj snorted. Whether it was in disbelief or in agreement was impossible to tell. But in response to the pressure of Lion's heels against his flanks, he made no further protest and set off in the direction of the ranch house as quickly as he could manage with two riders on his back.

Chapter 27

It was a quarter after five when Lion and Todd finally reached the ranch. In the distance a car had turned off the highway and was starting down the winding drive, but Lion hardly gave it a glance, for the important thing was that their station wagon was parked by the ranch house. "Dad's back!" he told Todd excitedly, not realizing till that moment how much he'd been counting on that.

Stopping just long enough to pull off Raj's saddle and bridle and pour a pint beaker of oats into a pail for him, they hurried as quickly as Todd could manage into the house.

The study door was open. Even as they started across the hall, they could hear Montcrief's angry voice saying "... this stalling has gone on long enough. My lawyer is here, and we wish to move on to settle the question of ownership of this ranch. I have a letter here, which my lawyer has prepared. I have asked him to read it to you."

By unspoken consent Todd and Lion stopped in the hallway to listen, still out of the sight of the people inside. There was the sound of a chair being pushed back, someone clearing his throat, then the lawyer's ponderous voice began, "My client and I are aware that the insurance company has not yet stated officially that the equipment shed fire on the Willow Creek Ranch was deliberately set by Todd Simpson in an effort to claim the insurance money by fraud or that he proved his guilt by subsequently running away. But the insurance company believes this to be true. Until they are convinced otherwise, they are withholding any settlement of the claim. Accordingly, the loan extended by Mr. Montcrief to enable Mr. Simpson to replace his ranch equipment remains in force, with three percent of the ranch shares being transferred over as a guarantee of good faith. That means that as of this moment, Mr.Montcrief and his future wife control fifty-one percent of the voting shares of Willow Creek Ranch and therefore assume full decision making powers —"

"But I didn't set the fire," Todd's quiet voice interrupted from the doorway. "And I didn't run away."

The lawyer stopped in mid-sentence.

There was a gasp of relief from Chrissy, who was sitting anxiously in the meeting.

Todd smiled at her warmly, then turned his attention to Montcrief. "However, I think I can prove who did set it." In spite of being close to exhaustion, his voice was firm. Again he turned to Chrissy. "Is my camera still out where we set it by the pond to run that test for our photo shoot?"

A guilty look replaced the relief on Chrissy's face. "I forgot! Oh, Todd, I'm sorry! I should have remembered we'd left it there! I should have brought it back, only with everything else that has been happening —"

"I'm glad you didn't," Todd told her. He paused for breath. "If you had, and if anyone had noticed you bringing it in, it might have disappeared like I would have if it hadn't been for a couple of pretty smart friends." He threw Lion and Bobbi a grateful grin, then turned back to Chrissy. "Will you go and get it now?"

Quickly she got to her feet and left the room. They could hear her footsteps in the hall as she hurried toward the door.

Todd returned his attention to Montcrief who for the first time was looking uncomfortable. "I put a long range lens on the camera then set it out about nine o'clock the night before the fire," he began. "When Chrissy returns she'll back me up on that. I put it out in that wide grassy area that runs in front of the big pond, positioned so the equipment shed was in the background to provide contrast and perspective." His face was grey with the strain of so much talking. "We set the timer on the shutter to take a picture every five minutes all night. That way we figured we'd catch any animals coming to the pond to drink."

As Montcrief realized what Todd was saying the colour slowly drained from his face.

"If anyone walked across the clearing that night and went into the equipment shed —" Todd went on, spacing the words carefully now, "they'll appear on that film. And since we were using a long distance lens, so might anything anybody was carrying — like a length of wire, for instance, or a jug of gasoline. Or perhaps even a wooden horse-clock."

Chapter 28

Todd was still managing to remain on his feet as Montcrief, Kurt and Montcrief's lawyer stalked off. As soon as they had disappeared, Brock Simpson was on his feet. Crossing the room in half a dozen quick strides, and not even trying to hide the tears that were streaming down his cheeks, he seized his son in a hug that Lion was sure would break all his ribs.

Todd grinned back at him fondly.

Chrissy burst back into the study carrying Todd's camera.

"It was exactly where we left it!" she exclaimed breathlessly, "And the whole role of film has been used up! We must have got lots of pictures!"

"Good," Dad said with relief. "Then we should have the proof we need."

But all at once Todd looked uncomfortable. "I just thought of something," he said sheepishly. "You know that automatic date stamp that you can set on cameras like this to record when each picture was taken? Well, it's a drag when I'm setting time exposures for animals that I want to draw, because it prints in big, white numbers across the lower right corner of each picture and often cuts out some really important detail that I need to see."

A funny look had come over Dad's face. "So, exactly what are you saying?"

"That when I'm taking snaps of animals to draw, I always turn the date stamp off."

Dad's face was unreadable. "Did you turn it off before you set your camera out in the field by the equipment shed?"

Numbly Todd nodded.

For the next little while, no one seemed to feel like talking — everyone seemed to be busy with their own thoughts. But at last Dad looked up. "I've been thinking about this whole business, Brock," he said carefully, "and wondering if we should consider settling out of court."

"But we can't let Montcrief get away with all the harm he's done!"

"No. But before we decide to take him to court, we should be fairly confident that we could win."

Mr. Simpson looked over sharply. "Are you saying we might find it hard to prove our case?"

Dad nodded. "There is very little real evidence. For example, we'd find it extremely difficult to prove that any of those so-called accidents were anything but accidents, for no one seems to have seen anything. As for the fire, if those films of Todd's aren't dated, a smart lawyer would have little trouble raising doubts in the court's mind as to whether or not the pictures could have been staged."

"But what about the attack on Todd?"

"Unfortunately, Todd never saw his assailant. There

is nothing to link either Montcrief or Kurt to any of this."

Lion moved closer to Bobbi. "That's true," he whispered. "We don't even know for sure who was down the basement that night when we were getting Break Away, because we didn't see him."

"As for who locked Todd up," Dad was continuing, "we've got to remember that he was locked in a shed on the Simpson's own property. There is nothing to suggest Montcrief had anything to do with it, because again nobody saw the assailant."

Mr. Simpson was frowning. "Are you saying we couldn't prove our case?"

"We probably could eventually, but it could mean months of expensive litigation and unpleasant publicity. The way the courts work nowadays with delays and appeals, a good part of the insurance money could be used up just paying legal fees."

Dad paused then went on, "This whole thing was carefully planned. There is nothing to link Montcrief or Kurt with any of it. All they need to do is manufacture some convincing poof that they were somewhere else at the time of the fire, and our case could fall apart."

"So what are you suggesting, Syd?" Mr. Simpson said quietly.

"That we take advantage of the fact that Todd's sudden and unexpected reappearance momentarily threw them off balance, and before they have time to recover, we back them into a corner."

"How?"

"First, I suggest we send a signed statement to the insurance company releasing them from any obligation to pay that insurance claim, so they will no longer be involved." Dad smiled. "I have an idea they'll be greatly relieved. Then, I suggest we confront Montcrief and insist that he immediately cancel that loan at the bank and deposit the full amount of the money involved into your account as payment for the equipment that he deliberately destroyed. Of course we'll also insist on the immediate return of the three percent of the ranch shares that he cleverly managed to have transferred to his name as collateral."

The grey, numb look started to fade from Mr. Simpson's face. He smiled. "Anything else?"

"Yes. I think we should insist that he put his place on the market and move out of the province. And we should also make it clear that we will not hesitate to reopen the issue and lay formal charges against him if there is ever any suggestion that he might be bending the law somewhere else."

As Dad had been talking, new footsteps had sounded in the hall, but since none of the others seemed to be paying any attention, Lion decided to ignore them, too. Besides, he wanted to hear what Mr. Simpson was going to answer.

For a moment Mr. Simpson continued to frown. "I agree with everything except the suggestion that we shouldn't make any of this public knowledge," he said carefully. "I know the publicity could be unpleasant, but

I have to tell Lani. And I have to tell her right way. I can't let her marry that guy tomorrow thinking he's a decent fellow —"

"It's all right, Brock," Lani said from the doorway.

That was who he'd heard coming back into the hall, Lion realized! And that's who owned that car he'd seen off in the distance, starting down toward the ranch. He should have recognized it, but at the time he'd been so relieved to see Dad's station wagon parked by the house, that he hadn't thought about anything else.

Lani continued into the room, her attention focused solely on Mr. Simpson. "I've known for weeks that I really didn't want to marry Warren," she went on as if no one else was even there. "That's what I came back to tell you. Even if I hadn't overheard what you were saying about him, I still wasn't going to marry him because —" she broke off in embarrassment, then finished with a shy smile. "Because how can I marry one person when I'm still in love with someone else?"

As the meaning of her words sank, in the worry and concern faded from Brock Simpson's face. He got to his feet. In the next moment he had taken Lani in his arms.

"Hey, terrific!" Todd said beaming.

Quickly, Lion looked over at Chrissy. Would she object?

To Lion's relief, Chrissy was beaming too.

Chapter 29

"Do you believe in space visitors?" Bobbi asked Dad next morning in an overly casual voice as they left Willow Creek Ranch and started back home.

Dad had been concentrating on piloting the station wagon and the horse trailer out the narrow ranch driveway, but now he looked over sharply. "Does that question mean you two managed to locate that crop circle?"

Bobbi nodded.

"And what did you decide? Are the people right who say it's just a prank?"

For a second neither Bobbi nor Lion answered.

Finally, Bobbi said instead, "You do believe there *could* be such things as space visitors, don't you Dad? I've heard you say lots of times that just because a person has never experienced something doesn't prove it isn't possible."

"True," Dad agreed but his voice sounded more joking than serious.

"So, *could* there be space visitors?" Bobbi insisted.

The amusement left Dad's face. He looked across the front seat carefully. "Have you and your brother met someone who was pretending to be a space visitor?"

"Not pretending. She didn't say anything about herself at all. But I'm positive there was something special about her. She seemed to be able to contact us just by thinking."

"Lots of people can do that, Hon."

"She also managed to turn up just when she was needed," Lion put in.

The amusement returned to Dad's eyes as he met Lion's glance in the overhead mirror. "Don't tell me you believe she was a space visitor too."

"I didn't say that!" Lion defended quickly. "I just mean it's weird how she kept turning up."

"But do you think there really *could* be space visitors, Dad?" Bobbi insisted again.

For a long moment, Dad didn't answer. Then he said carefully, "Let's put it this way: I don't personally believe in that sort of thing, but I heard something yesterday concerning that crop circle, and I think it will interest you. It seems a couple of Mr. Simpson's neighbors were the first ones to spot it. They'd been out on horseback checking the fence lines and all of a sudden saw the pattern in the distance. They were sure it hadn't been there a little while earlier when they'd come down the other side of that same open meadow, so they decided to ride over and investigate. Only they had such a time trying to control their horses they had to give it up. The horses refused to go near. They were so terrified, they nearly bolted. And the cattle dog they had with them took off for home. The men claimed it wasn't till they'd turned around and were a good hundred metres away that the horses finally settled down."

Bobbi's face was shining. "Then there *was* electricity there when the crop circle first appeared! That proves it!"

Again, Dad smiled across the front seat. He shook his head. "I'm afraid it doesn't. It could have been the scent of a bear or a cougar that was scaring the horses."

It was true, Lion realized. To his surprise he was kind of disappointed. It would have been neat if that girl really had been a space visitor. But Dad was right. It was much more likely that those men's horses had been scared by the smell of a bear or a cougar.

He settled back in the seat. "Even if that girl wasn't from space," he said aloud, "she was still pretty smart. What she said about that Aristotle guy really worked."

"Who?" Dad asked in a disbelieving voice, his eyes once again meeting Lion's in the overhead mirror.

"Aristotle. This really hotshot philosopher guy who she claimed lived two thousand three hundred years ago."

"I am well aware of who Aristotle was," Dad replied at his driest. "But I hadn't realized you were. Which makes me grateful to this girl, whether she was a space visitor or not. Anyone who can get you talking about philosophers instead of baseball players has my undying thanks."

Lion grinned. "She said that way back in 350 BC this guy said nothing happened except something else happened first, and he was right. That's how we worked out where Todd was hidden."

Again Dad glanced back at Lion in the overhead mirror. A new thoughtful look had come into his eyes. "Then I'm delighted you talked to her. Also," he added, and the amusement crept back, "I'm glad she pointed out to you that nothing happens except something else happens first. Because as soon as we get home, you have a week's gardening to do."

"Gardening!" Lion protested. More than anything else in the whole world he hated gardening. "Come on, Dad, why?"

"To pay for that kitchen window," Dad answered simply.

At that Bobbi came out of her reverie. She burst out laughing.

With a disgruntled sigh, Lion settled back in his seat. He'd forgotten all about that window. Why couldn't he pay for it some other way than by gardening?

But at that moment, a new thought struck and he felt better. With any luck, if this coming week was like every other week so far this summer, within a day or two Dad would be called to go and solve another case somewhere. When he did, maybe he'd let them go with him again. After all, he must realize by now how much he needed them. In which case a couple of days of gardening probably wouldn't be so bad.

Besides, he told himself, it had been a really neat homer. A guy had to be prepared to do something in return.

About the Author

Joan Weir is an accomplished writer for young readers with an impressive list of books to her credit. In addition to the other two books in the Lion and Bobbi series, she has published *Sixteen is Spelled O-U-C-H* (Stoddart, 1996) and *Mystery at Lighthouse Rock* (Stoddart, 1991). Joan Weir teaches creative writing at the University College of the Cariboo and lives in Kamloops, British Columbia, where she rides her horse Raj — the model for Lion's feisty horse in the mystery series.

Other books in the Lion and Bobbi Mystery Series:

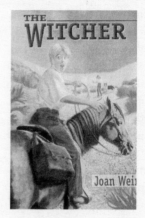

The Witcher
Joan Weir
"Take an intriguing title, add a mystery, include a dash of danger, a bantering family and a hate-love relationship with a horse, and you've got the ingredients for a book that will please a wide-ranging audience. *The Witcher* will hook young readers." — *Quill & Quire*
ISBN 1-896095-44-5
$8.95 CDN / $5.95 USA

The Principal's Kid
Joan Weir
The second book in the best-selling Lion and Bobbi mystery series. Nominated for the Silver Birch Award, and winner of the BC 2000 Book Award.
ISBN 1-896095-98-4
$8.95 CDN / $5.95 USA

Bright Lights from Polestar

Polestar Books, an imprint of Raincoast Books, takes pride in creating books that introduce discriminating readers to exciting writers. These independent voices illuminate our histories and engage our imaginations.

More Books for Teens and Young Adults from Polestar: